Your Killin' Heart

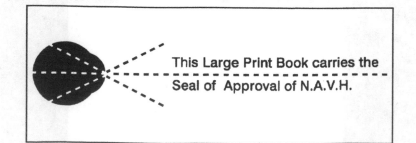

This Large Print Book carries the
Seal of Approval of N.A.V.H.

A NASHVILLE MYSTERY

Your Killin' Heart

Peggy O'Neal Peden

WHEELER PUBLISHING
A part of Gale, a Cengage Company

Farmington Hills, Mich • San Francisco • New York • Waterville, Maine
Meriden, Conn • Mason, Ohio • Chicago

LIBRARY OF CONGRESS CIP DATA ON FILE.
CATALOGUING IN PUBLICATION FOR THIS BOOK
IS AVAILABLE FROM THE LIBRARY OF CONGRESS

ISBN-13: 978-1-4328-4272-7 (softcover)
ISBN-10: 1-4328-4272-2 (softcover)

Published in 2017 by arrangement with Macmillan Publishing Group, LLC/St. Martin's Press

Printed in Mexico
1 2 3 4 5 6 7 21 20 19 18 17

To Mom and Dad,
Mark and Mike, and, of course,
David

The last lonesome train
is takin' me home;
I've been on this highway too long.
Will anyone there remember my name
Or hear the pain in my song?
— Jake Miller, "Last Lonesome Train"

CHAPTER ONE

He was an icon in country music. He had written heartbreaking songs and sung them from a heart full of pain and self-imposed demons. Then he'd had the good business sense to die young — and somewhat mysteriously.

The Grand Ole Opry had turned down Jake Miller when he had tried to join, but now all the old-timers in Nashville talked as if they'd been his best friends. His brief career and life were enshrined in a museum case of revisionist memories, the truth as carefully filtered as too much moisture or sunlight.

My dad was a big fan. He played guitar. Who doesn't around Nashville? And, as a young man, he had been in a band, just a few guys who would get together on weekends and play, their wives sitting bored in the kitchen waiting for them to get tired and go home. But it took a long time for them to get tired of picking Jake Miller songs.

That's why I begged to go along. I just didn't expect to find a body.

My friend Doug Elliott had mentioned that he had to pick up — sounded better than "repossess" — some paintings for his brother's gallery. The Mockingbird Gallery, named for the Tennessee state bird, because the gallery focused on local artists.

"Why you?" I asked.

"You know Ken," Doug said. "If there's dirty work, let somebody else do it. I think he thinks people are intimidated because I'm a lawyer. He can apologize for me later, maybe still keep the client. It might be tricky. It's Hazel Miller."

"Hazel Miller? Jake Miller's Hazel Miller?"

"Campbell . . ."

"I could help. It'll be easier with a woman there."

"Nothing is ever easier with you there, Campbell Hale."

I was shocked. I was hurt. At least, those were the looks I was going for. Doug rolled his eyes.

"You need a woman with you. Good cop, bad cop."

"Campbell . . ." He was shaking his head

by then. "You'll be working." He was triumphant. He'd found an excuse.

"No, no, I'm off tomorrow." I'm a travel agent. I manage an agency in Nashville's Hillsboro Village, an area centered along Twenty-first Avenue that still has a neighborhood identity and personality. It borders the Vanderbilt University medical complex, not far from Music Row, Green Hills, and a couple of other college campuses. Students and businesspeople rub shoulders with health-care professionals and music types. A great place to work, but I had the day off. "I can help carry. Surely you can use an extra pair of hands," I pleaded. "I won't break anything. I won't even speak without your permission. How many chances does a person get to see inside Jake Miller's house?"

I wanted to be able to tell my dad about the interior of Jake Miller's last home. Jake Miller's widow, a second or third wife, still lived in the house they'd built with the profits from his biggest hit, "Last Lonesome Train." Jake might have played a sad guitar, but Hazel Miller played Nashville for all it was worth. She was always there at music-industry awards dinners, smiling vaguely through an alcoholic haze, accepting a plaque and thanking "the people" for keeping Jake's memory alive — and buying his records and the records of newer stars who kept rerecording his old songs. They not only kept his memory alive; they kept his estate prosperous.

At least, everybody assumed the estate was prosperous. Hazel lived in a mansion behind a high brick wall on Franklin Road. Her gowns dripped rhinestones and sequins. Her cars were huge and gaudy.

"I might not even get inside," Doug said. "I'm just picking up these paintings for Ken. Six paintings. She bought them but never paid him. I can't believe he let them out the door without money in his hand, personally. They're supposed to be expecting me, so they might just have them sitting by the door."

"Please."

He sighed. "If I tell you to go sit in the car, you go sit in the car."

And I knew I had won.

"Absolutely. You're the boss."

He didn't believe it, but I'd worn him down. "Okay," he finally agreed. "Just don't gush."

It wasn't like I'd ever really caused him harm. Sometimes I'd say the wrong thing around his friends. Sometimes I was a little too honest. How bad a character flaw is

12

that? Bad enough, apparently, to avoid committing to a relationship but not horrible enough for him to avoid me altogether. I crossed my heart.

It was late afternoon as we drove south on Franklin Road, the sunroof open to let in the sunny and warm, perfect fall day. Doug kept his eyes on the road. I split my attention between the scenery and Doug. Gray-blue eyes, six feet tall, fit from running three days a week. Doug's brown hair was the only unruly thing about him.

Birds flitted in the trees that reached over the road. It was too late in the year for songbirds, but the mockingbirds aren't tourists. They stay with us all year, flying in pairs, teasing and flirting from branch to branch, singing songs borrowed from the other birds. Doing covers, I suppose they'd say in the industry, recording their own versions of someone else's song. My neighbor, Mr. Morgan, had a favorite mockingbird story. He was working construction and waiting for a dump truck to get out of his way. The dump truck made its distinctive *beep, beep* sound as it backed up. "That truck shifted into forward," he said, "and drove off, but I kept hearin' that same *beep, beep, beep.* I thought somethin' was wrong with my hearin', from all the blastin'. I kept hearin' it, and that truck got farther away, then out of sight. I finally looked around and saw a mockingbird. It was imitatin' the dump truck. A bird imitatin' a truck! Durndest thing I ever saw."

Leaves skittered across the road, pressing up against the fences like eager fans trying to get a glimpse of a star. Nashvillians are generally blasé about their country music stars. You see them in restaurants, on the street, at Target. Your kids play Little League with their kids. You see Tim and Faith at Ensworth games. You may smile and nod so they don't get insecure, tell them you liked their last song — if it hasn't been too long since their last song. But a native never gawks. Still, I was excited. I'd spent too many years listening to my daddy play Jake's songs not to be thrilled at the prospect of being inside that house.

Doug turned off the road and stopped in front of tall iron gates. He pressed a button beside the speaker at his window, and out came a squawk that seemed to contain a question. Doug must have understood, because he responded, "Doug Elliott. I'm from The Mockingbird Gallery. Mrs. Miller is expecting me."

After a moment of silence, there was

another squawk, and the gates began to open. The driveway curved up a gentle slope. The landscaping was elaborate and not exactly seedy, but there was an aura of early neglect. There were weeds in the daylily beds, and the juniper ground cover bordering the drive seemed to have scribbled out of the lines.

"I have a friend who has a theory about the economics of trees," I said. "His hobby is horticulture, and he thinks that trees determine the property values of neighborhoods. Maples are middle class; oaks and magnolias are upper. What do you think?"

Doug said nothing.

I keep looking for yards that disprove his theory, but this wasn't one of them. The oaks and magnolias were there instead of the maples that blazed in my neighborhood, plus weeping cherry and discreet ground covers. Someone had put a lot of expense and care into this garden once.

There was a pea-gravel parking area to the right side of the entrance, but Doug stopped in front of the door. "Not as far to carry the paintings," he explained. I nodded.

At the elaborately carved door, Doug pushed another button. Chimes rang inside the house. We waited. Doug was calm, as

15

always. He's not impressed by much. I'm not even sure just how impressed he is with me. He doesn't give much away.

The door remained closed. Doug pressed the button once more, and again we heard chimes but no approaching footsteps.

"If they didn't want to let us in, they wouldn't have opened the gate, would they?" I asked.

"I don't like this," Doug said. "Ken said she agreed to give them back, but if she's changed her mind, there's nothing I can do. Even though she hasn't paid for them, Ken doesn't have a lien on them."

"I thought Ken said he talked to Hazel today," I said.

"He talked to her two weeks ago. Today he confirmed this appointment with the personal assistant. A man named George Lewis."

Doug pressed the button once more and looked impatiently at his watch. Then we heard footsteps. A maid opened the door. She seemed a little flustered and out of breath.

"Good afternoon." Her dark chocolate skin gleamed, and she wore a crisp black uniform topped by a white apron.

"I'm Doug Elliott. May I see Mrs. Miller, please? She's expecting me. We're from The

16

Mockingbird Gallery."

"Oh, yes." She seemed relieved. "Miz Miller is not available."

"But I have an appointment. She's expecting me."

"Yes, sir, I know. You're here for the pictures, but you can't see Miz Miller. She's not available." She held the door wide, and we stepped into the entry. It was spacious with rooms opening to the right, left, and rear. A highly polished cherry staircase curved its way upstairs. Matching Chippendale settees upholstered in gold tapestry stood at opposite walls. There was just a little too much gold in the wallpaper, a little too much of everything. It was hard to put a finger on, but it gave me the impression of expensive tackiness. Just because you have money doesn't mean you have good taste. Maybe that was why Kenneth hadn't wanted to come. He would take anybody's money, but he hated to see good art surrounded by poor taste.

Mrs. Miller's taste in art, though, seemed very good, or else she had listened to a very discriminating advisor. I recognized the work of a nationally known sculptor and a very good — and expensive — local one. I nudged Doug and raised an eyebrow.

"I really don't want to take the paintings

17

without talking with Mrs. Miller," he was saying.

"Oh, it's all right. She knew you was coming. I'll show you right where they are."

"Well, thank you. I appreciate your help, but I really need to talk to Mrs. Miller."

The maid seemed uneasy at Doug's insistence. "Yes, sir, but she can't talk right now. She said you was just to take the paintings. He said for me to help you."

"He?"

"Yes, sir. Mr. Lewis. He's Miz Miller's personal assistant. He said I was to help you."

Doug looked stymied. He liked things to be neat, with no loose ends. He followed the rules and was very thorough. It was one of the qualities I counted on him for. I could talk to him — and often did — about a situation, and he would think it through with me. You could watch his clear blue eyes and almost see the gears turning, meshing, setting off other motions. He would look at the question from every possible angle, mentally play out every possible consequence, then tell you what he thought. He had a hard time with spontaneity, but he made up for it in reliability. Doug was a man you could count on.

"We'll wait," he announced.

The maid seemed flustered.

"Sir, I don't want no trouble. Miz Miller said I was to show you the pictures. Can't you just take them?"

"We'll wait."

The maid must have recognized a brick wall when she tried to argue with one, so she said, "Yes, sir," and left us in the entrance hall.

We sat on the Chippendale settee against the left wall.

I was taking in the details, already rehearsing what I would tell my dad. Doug looked uncomfortable. I smiled reassuringly. He scowled.

We waited.

"I wish I could wander around some," I said.

Doug looked sideways at me, not responding.

"I mean, Jake Miller! I know he only lived here the last few years of his life, but still, there was some great songwriting in this house."

Doug still said nothing.

"Wouldn't you like to see his favorite spot for writing, where he liked to sit and play guitar maybe? Really? Somewhere deep inside?"

"I knew this would happen. I shouldn't

have let you come."

"I'm not doing anything wrong. I'm sitting here behaving. I'm just talking, making conversation, sharing a small part of my dreams, my heart, my soul."

Doug almost smiled. "This is not going the way it was supposed to. Maybe you'd better hang onto your soul right now. You don't want to leave anything lying around if we have to make a fast getaway."

I nodded. "What's your favorite Jake Miller song?"

He shrugged. "I'm not much of a country-music fan."

"I know, but everybody knows Jake Miller songs. 'Last Lonesome Train'? 'Saturday Night in Town'? 'Tomorrow Again'?"

Doug shrugged again.

"Is this what you thought it would be like? His house, I mean?"

He looked surprised, then shook his head. "I hadn't thought anything about it."

I knew he was telling the truth. No imagination. That's a blessing sometimes. Doug would never imagine all the crazy things that could possibly go wrong the way I always did.

"I guess I thought it would be a little more . . . I don't know . . . or maybe not so much . . ." I didn't know what to say. "It kind of looks like it was decorated thirty years ago and hasn't been touched since. Except that she was buying art from Ken."

Doug nodded, but he still didn't make conversation. He was on task.

After a little more than half an hour, a young man, thirtyish, in jeans, a heavily starched white shirt, boots, and a blazer entered the hall from behind us.

"Sorry you've been waiting all this time. Did Estelle tell you to go ahead and take the paintings? I'm George Lewis, Mrs. Miller's personal assistant."

"Doug Elliott. This is Campbell Hale." We all shook hands.

"Nice to meet you both. I'm really sorry that Mrs. Miller won't be able to see you. She hasn't been feeling well, and she's asleep. We really can't . . . well, we don't want to wake her when she's resting."

Doug fidgeted, impatient.

"Look, she wants you to pick up the paintings," Lewis continued. "There's no question about that. And there's really no need for you to waste your time and come back another day. I'll help you get them to your car, okay?"

Doug still looked undecided, but I could see him glancing at the door. He was wavering.

"You're sure that Mrs. Miller is aware that we were coming today?"

"Oh, yes. She just hasn't been well."

"And you're authorized to turn the paintings over to us? You'll sign a release?"

"Absolutely. No problem. Do you know the paintings?"

"Yes. I have a list and photographs."

"Great. I think I know which ones they are, but that will help. I know one's in the sitting room, but a couple are straight back in the music room. Why don't you and Miss Hale get those?"

Without waiting for an answer, Lewis headed back in the direction he had come, cowboy bootheels clacking on the marble floor.

Doug and I looked at each other.

"Straight back, the man said," I offered. "The music room." I smiled. "I guess that's this way."

We walked to the rear of the entrance hall toward a pair of double doors. We stopped, glanced at each other again, and each reached for a handle. We pulled open the doors and gasped. Well, Doug gasped; I screamed.

There in the center of the dark music room, in the light of a single spotlight, stood Jake Miller.

It wasn't really him, of course. It was an eerily lifelike wax sculpture of Jake looking for all the world as if he were about to sing "Last Lonesome Train." I almost expected him to tip his hat and say howdy to us. An old, worn Martin guitar waited in a stand near his right hand.

When my heart slowed down and I could breathe again, I looked sideways at Doug. He's rarely shaken by anything, or at least he rarely shows it. But Jake Miller had taken him by surprise, too. Doug's eyes were wide as he turned to me.

"Do you suppose there's another light in here?"

"Wait a second." I walked over to the statue, stopping about a yard away. My hand went out, almost involuntarily. Up close, the illusion faded, and, as Doug found a light switch, the brightness made the statue appear just that. I decided I preferred the view in the dark, the spotlight blurring the flat and lifeless lines. "They must have given it to Hazel when the wax museum downtown closed." The sequined suit looked tired, cleaned and pressed but obviously old. A suit Jake Miller had actually worn, singing in a real spotlight. The finish of the guitar was worn through where Jake Miller's fingers had strummed.

The room was a large one, with heavily draped windows and French doors lining the mansion's back wall. Jake Miller memorabilia covered the other walls, photographs of Jake with a governor, two presidents, famous Opry stars. There were several of Jake and his daughter Jackie, only a small child when her father died. There were gold records and platinum ones, with brass plaques detailing the years and sales. Other awards, many of which had to have been given after Jake's death, filled in the gaps. Whenever I looked back at the wax statue, its eyes seemed to follow me around the room. I knew it was just a statue, but it made me feel uneasy

"Look, Doug, it's the gold record for 'Last Lonesome Train.' His whole career is here. This one is 'The Sound of My Heart Breakin.' This is great. Wait until I tell my dad."

"Yes, but where are the paintings?"

I then remembered why we had come — or at least why Doug had come — and scanned the room. On one end was a large, superrealistic painting of the bridge of a guitar. I thought that might be one we were looking for and went over to examine it. I eased the lower edge of the gilt frame out from the wall to look at the back. A gold sticker bore the name and address of the gallery and the trademark mockingbird in flight.

"Here's one," I said. Doug was busy examining the few items on the wall that were not relics of Jake's career. An abstract of Jake and early Opry legends hung on the opposite wall. Doug ignored the painting of Jake on black velvet that hung near the door, but I kind of liked it. He was ignoring the ones he thought couldn't possibly have come from Kenneth's gallery. I could imagine a triptych of Jake, Elvis, and the black-velvet Pancho Villa that hung in my favorite Mexican restaurant. Not why we were here, though. "You're right, this is one, too."

Doug was lifting the abstract from its hanger. He handed it to me. "He did say there were just two in here, right?" Doug shuffled through his photographs.

"Right. These others don't have the gallery sticker on the back."

"Okay. Let's see what else there is." Doug took down the guitar-bridge painting and started for the door.

"Wait, Doug. Let me look around another minute." I walked around the room's perimeter, peering again at the memorabilia on the walls, and returned to face the wax sculpture. There was a half smile, and the glass eyes looked into a distance beyond the crowds, beyond the beer bottles on the tables. The fingers of its left hand curved as if to make a G chord on the neck of a guitar; the right thumb was poised as if to strum. "It's sad, isn't it? His life reduced to this room?"

"I guess. But not too many people these days have their own shrines."

"True. It just seems as if it's almost too insistent, as if they're trying to convince themselves that he really was here, really had a life and was a star, and it all meant something."

"It's about money. You create a mystique; it sells better."

"You have no imagination, you know."

"That's what they tell me. I think I had to send in my imagination with the fee before I took the bar exam."

"And you're a cynic."

"Thank you. Let's go."

"Okay, but help me remember all this stuff so I can tell my dad. I should have brought my phone in so I could take pictures."

Doug rolled his eyes. "Fine. Can you get the door?"

Doug and I set the two paintings in the entrance hall. George Lewis came back carrying another, a small floral abstract. "There are three more, right?"

Doug nodded.

"I'll show you another, Mr. Elliott. Then I'll get the other two while you take these out to your car."

Doug followed Lewis, and I was left alone in the entrance hall. This was my chance. With one last look in the direction they had gone, I turned and wandered down the opposite hall. The first room I came to was a sitting room, cool and forbidding, furnished all in beiges. Beyond that, through a wide arch, was a large, formal dining room with hunter-green walls and hunt-print wallpaper above a chair rail. A short hallway turned to the left and I followed it. A single door was at the end of the hall.

I'm not usually this nosy in someone else's home, but this was Jake Miller's house. I opened the door into a dim, draped room before I realized it was a bedroom. I had a quick impression of soft greens, floral prints, and an old woman, still and silent on the bed. Hazel's bedroom? I closed the door quickly and quietly so I wouldn't wake her and stole back to the entrance hall, scared to death that the housekeeper or, worse, Doug would catch me.

I hadn't expected to find a bedroom downstairs in this house. As I looked at that staircase, curving so impressively up to what surely were the bedrooms, I wondered if a downstairs room had been converted for Hazel since her health had worsened.

The entrance hall still empty, I slipped back into the music room for one last look at the statue, lit just by the spotlight. I was fascinated by the statue, but I thought it might be a little freaky to live with. I closed the door and went back to sit on my settee.

Doug returned a few minutes later with another painting. At a glance it seemed to be French Impressionist. By the time we had wrapped and loaded the four paintings, Lewis was back with the rest. We were loading those into the car when an old pickup truck skidded to a stop inches from Doug's car, spraying all of us with gravel. Two mockingbirds scattered in alarm. The pickup had apparently once been sky blue, now faded with age and too many close encounters with other Nashville drivers.

Lewis muttered under his breath as a young man in jeans, a denim jacket, and several earrings jumped from the truck. An empty pierced nostril suggested that this visit didn't rate the nose ring.

"You can't keep me out. She has to see me," he yelled.

"She's not seeing anybody today," Lewis

told him. "Look, settle down. Let me get ri— uh, help these people finish up, and we'll talk."

I could take a hint, so I told Lewis that it had been nice meeting him and got into the car. Doug got the release form out of his briefcase and handed it to Lewis to sign.

The boy fumed. His hair was long, dirty, and scraggly; his cowboy boots were old and scuffed; the wallet in his back pocket was attached by a chain. Lewis was distracted, obviously wanting to be rid of us. He signed the release without reading it.

The boy had started yelling again as Doug slid into the driver's seat. "I'm not taking this anymore. I have rights here, and you can't stop me."

We took the paintings back to the gallery. Kenneth's black Mercedes — diesel, of course, because that made it different, more European — was the only car in the lot. The Mockingbird Gallery was closed, but Kenneth was standing in the open door, waiting for us. I held doors and let Kenneth and Doug do the heavy work.

"Thanks, Doug," Kenneth said. "I'm glad to have them back. Did she give you a hard time?"

"We never saw her. The maid and the

29

personal assistant, Lewis, said she was resting. Lewis signed a release, but I'd feel better about it if I'd talked to her."

"George Lewis?"

"Yes."

Ken nodded. "You didn't break and enter, did you? No felonies were committed?"

Doug didn't laugh.

While they hoisted in the last of the paintings, I leaned against my hand on Ken's Mercedes hood, but jumped away. It was hot. Radiant heat, I guessed. The afternoon sun was fading, but most of the day had been hot for October and there was little shade in the lot. This had been one of the hottest summers in decades with a near-record stretch of days with highs over ninety.

"Thanks, guys," Kenneth said. "I'd take you to dinner, but I've got to dash home and pick up Carey and the kids. The kids are in a program at school tonight, but your dinner's on me, okay?"

"Don't worry," Doug assured him. "You're paying for dinner, all right. I'll send you a bill tomorrow."

Kenneth grimaced, then forced a grin and waved as he got into his Mercedes. The heavy engine roared. I realized he hadn't spoken a word directly to me.

Nevertheless, dinner was delicious. We

went to Maggiano's, my choice. It was late by the time we were seated, and I was hungry. "Let's have an appetizer while we wait." Doug grinned. "Ken would want us to." Doug ordered veal Parmesan; I had linguine with an Alfredo sauce that defied description. Doug nodded to a few acquaintances: a judge and a couple of state senators. The state legislature was in session.

I expected Doug to run for office sometime. When I asked him about it, he'd always shrug, but I knew he'd considered it. He'd been active in at least a couple of recent campaigns, working for candidates I couldn't in good conscience vote for. It was a shame, really. He was such a good man, but when it came to politics, we could never agree. I'd learned to avoid the whole subject. When he finally did run for office, I just hoped it wasn't in my district, so I wouldn't have to vote against him.

"Those paintings just didn't seem to fit in that house," I said. "You know I'm a fan of black velvet, but even I wouldn't hang Elvis anywhere near those paintings we picked up. I don't get it."

"She probably only had the black-velvet painting because it was of Jake." Doug shrugged. "Memorabilia. Ken's known her for a long time. I'm not sure how they met, but I guess she took his advice about art. He wouldn't have given her decorating advice, though. People have strange tastes."

"I guess."

"Besides, she probably had her house decorated years ago, when there was plenty of money. There hasn't been plenty of money for a long time."

"There was money enough for some very expensive art."

"She never paid for it," Doug pointed out. "That's why Ken sent me to pick up the paintings."

"True," I agreed. "They seemed out of place."

"Maybe that's why she decided not to keep them. Maybe she just decided she didn't want them. And I don't blame her. Some of that stuff . . . How can they call it art if you can't even tell what it is?"

"If you just want a picture, you can use a camera. Art is about color and space," I insisted, "about feeling. . . ."

We argued about modern and postmodern art until the waiter brought our entrees. I was distracted then because the Alfredo sauce was the best I'd ever tasted.

The first time I met Doug was the day his divorce became final. He'd stopped in at the Hillsboro Village–area travel agency that

I manage on his way back to his office from the courthouse. He was looking for escape, and that's mostly what I sell. He wasn't looking for a place to meet women; he just wanted to get away, put his life in perspective. It's a principle of mine never to make snap judgments about mistreated, vulnerable men and their horrid ex-wives, but his pain was real. I could see it.

I personally think there's no better place than a beach to put your life in perspective, except maybe on a boat. There's something cleansing in God's endless washing of the beach. Every morning it's fresh, and every morning it's there. I like the salty smell and the feel of sand on my bare feet and the sounds of the ocean, the boat halyards and the gulls. I can't go too long without feeling like Melville's Ishmael in *Moby-Dick:* "growing grim about the mouth" and deciding it's "high time to get to sea as soon as I can." I like the seafood, too, of course.

So I told Doug about my favorite beach, a little town outside of Destin on the Florida panhandle. It's a carefully planned resort town, with pastel houses like a postmodern interpretation of a New England fishing village. There are widow's walks and cupolas, screened-in porches and lazy fans. The restaurants are good; there's deep-sea fishing; and it's out of the way.

Describing the town to Doug made me want to go back; it was another gray February day in Nashville, and I was feeling a little drizzly in my own soul. It's a short flight from Nashville to the nearest airport, Panama City, or you can drive it in less than a day, if you want. I found Doug a decent airfare, made reservations with a well-recommended charter fishing guide, and booked him there for a week.

When he returned, he called to thank me and asked me to dinner. Something connected. I had a feeling of gears finally sliding into place. Something about us fit. But real life is complicated. I don't know if Doug's fear of getting too close came from the divorce or contributed to it, but we seemed stuck in some awkward forward-backward dance.

After dinner, we cuddled up on the couch at my house on the Cumberland River to watch television when the ten o'clock news came on. I remember thinking that things were going too well, that it must be time for one of Doug's disappearing acts. Whenever our relationship seems to be moving somewhere, whenever we seem to be approaching some small sense of commitment, Doug disappears for a while. I tried not to think about it. I'd made coffee, and we were sitting there, comfortable and relaxed. Then the lead story got our attention.

"Hazel Miller, widow of country legend Jake Miller, was found dead this evening in her home on Franklin Road. We go live to Dan Hansen at the scene."

"Police are investigating the death today of Hazel Miller, widow of country-music legend Jake Miller. Mrs. Miller's body was discovered this evening at her home here on Franklin Road." The young reporter gestured past the yellow police tape to the shockingly familiar front door. I'd just been there. "She was apparently found by members of the household staff." There was film of George Lewis talking to police on the front steps.

"Police are not commenting on the investigation. While the death may have been from natural causes, they say nothing has been ruled out at this point, including the possibility of foul play."

I turned to Doug. "What are we going to do?"

"What do you mean?"

"Well, we were there! Our fingerprints are all over. And we saw that boy having a fit at the entrance as we were leaving."

"What's that got to do with anything? We

don't know anything. We didn't see Hazel Miller. We don't know what happened or when or how. We don't have anything to tell."

"But Doug, we were right there. We could even be suspects."

"Suspects for what? For all we know — or anybody knows right now — she died in her sleep."

"Doug! I saw her."

"You saw who?"

"I saw Hazel. At least, I might have seen her."

"What are you talking about?"

"When you were gone with that Lewis guy. I went down the other hall, and I saw her."

"She was in the hallway?"

"No . . ."

"Where was she? More to the point, where were *you*?"

"I . . . just kind of opened a door, and there she was."

"Did she speak to you?"

"No. Well, she didn't see me."

"Didn't see you?"

"She was in bed. Asleep. I thought." Could I have done something then? I thought she was asleep and didn't want to disturb her, but what if I had gone for help?

Could someone have resuscitated her then?

"Let me get this straight. You went snooping in her bedroom?"

"I didn't know it was her bedroom. It didn't seem like someplace you'd find a bedroom. I just thought I'd look around a little. Nobody was around. I wasn't going to bother anything."

"Campbell! You were in somebody's home! And you were sneaking around in it!"

"Well, I'm sorry! I was quiet and shut the door really quick. I didn't disturb her."

He raised an eyebrow. "Was she alive?"

"Oh, Doug! I don't know. She was lying in the bed. I thought she was asleep. It was just a second. And I don't know for sure it was even her. I couldn't see that well. The room was dark. What should we do?"

"There's nothing for us to do. You don't want to get messed up in something like this. If anybody decides to question us, then just tell the truth, answer their questions. But don't go looking for trouble."

"You're right. I just don't want to be hauled away for obstructing justice."

"I don't see how it could be a big deal. She died in her sleep. Besides, you know a good lawyer," Doug said. "Don't forget they have to let you make a phone call."

"Yes, but what if they already have you?"

"Could be a problem." He dismissed my concern. "Look, I've got to be in court in the morning. I'll talk to you tomorrow. I'll let you know what the gossip is."

Then I called my best friend MaryNell.

CHAPTER TWO

Do you call out my name when you're
   crying?
Do you miss me when rain chills your soul?
                              — Jake Miller,
           "The Sound of My Heart Breakin' "

The gossip at the courthouse and in the lunch-crowded restaurants on Second Avenue the next day was that Hazel Miller had died in the company of one of her closest companions — Jack Daniels. She'd been drinking and using drugs — nothing illegal: prescription sleeping pills, antidepressants — and the combination had killed her. No real surprise. Her drinking habits had been common rumor for years. She had stumbled across more than one stage.

Something smelled fishy, though, said an assistant district attorney Doug had gone to law school with. Hazel had apparently been dead for several hours. The maid and personal assistant had been in the house the whole time. In Tennessee, all deaths without a medical authority have to be investigated to determine if they're from natural causes, suicide, or homicide. Routine. But because she was who she was, they couldn't afford to make any mistakes. There would be too much attention. The fans with inquiring minds would want to know how a staff of servants could have failed to notice that the poor bereaved woman had left this earth and gone to be with Jake. There was probably nothing there, but if the police and the DA's office didn't go over everything with a fine-tooth comb, the national tabloids would. One of the late-night tabloid television shows was already running a promo spot linking Hazel's death to her husband's.

Everybody in my office had a theory. Martha thought the housekeeper did it; in lieu of a butler, Anna was convinced that the personal assistant was the murderer. Lee said we should all get lives and leave the poor woman and her family alone. I thought we should all get back to work. I had a client in London whose purse had been stolen with her passport and credit cards inside. Luckily, she had taken my advice and packed a copy of her passport in her luggage. In between providing details of the flocked wallpaper in Hazel's house, I was faxing and e-mailing information about the US embassy in London to her hotel. I was also calling her credit-card companies. Not a part of my job description, but it was something I could do to help. I couldn't give her back the time out of her first trip to London that she was going to waste getting her passport replaced, though.

At lunchtime I called home to tell my parents about my visit to Jake Miller's house.

"It was pretty cool, Dad. There was a wax sculpture, and its eyes looked like they were following me around the room. His guitars were there. That Martin you see in a lot of the pictures, it was there."

"They're saying Hazel was murdered."

"Yeah, Daddy, but it's probably just gossip. She wasn't in good health, and she drank too much."

"Well, you be careful," my mother said from the other extension. "To think you might have been there when something was going on!"

"Oh, no, Mom. We were just there a few minutes. It's really nothing to do with me." But it felt like it was something to do with me. It felt weird to think I'd seen Hazel in her bed, and shortly after that she was dead.

We talked a few minutes, but I knew I would need to tell Daddy all the details later. It seemed a little cold to be dissing the woman's decorating when she had just died.

"You take care of yourself," Mom said. "Be careful."

"I will. Y'all, too."

My parents and I were in that delicate in-between stage. They were concerned about my safety. After all, I was a single woman living alone in a city where dangerous things occasionally happened. And I worried about them. They were getting older but still climbing ladders and trees, still doing everything they could and a few things they couldn't. My mother kept trying to get my daddy to call a plumber when anything went wrong with pipes, but he still had to try to fix it himself first. Then he called a plumber to clean up his mess.

We weren't long past the time when they took care of me, when Daddy would come once in a while to handle whatever mainte-nance my house needed, but I could tell we also weren't far from the time when we'd be reversing those roles. In the meantime, we all told each other to be careful. I guess we all worried.

That afternoon a police detective came by

the office. Sam Davis.

"Sam Davis? Like the Boy Hero of the Confederacy?" I asked.

"That's right. Except older and still alive."

"You probably get that a lot, don't you? I've been to his house in Smyrna, seen the window he climbed through on his last visit home."

Sam Davis was a Confederate scout, hanged as a spy at the age of nineteen because he was captured wearing a Union overcoat that his mother had dyed brown with walnut hulls so he could survive the winter. That overcoat meant he could be held — and executed — as a spy by Union forces. He could have saved himself if he had revealed the source of his intelligence or that his leader was being held in the same stockade in Pulaski, Tennessee, but in the tradition of young men in a thousand wars, he chose to die with honor.

"Yes, ma'am. Not so much, really. I've got just a few routine questions, ma'am. Your name was given to us by several people, including Kenneth Elliott. We understand you went to Hazel Miller's residence yesterday with Doug Elliott representing Elliott's art gallery."

He paused. I didn't say anything. There didn't seem to be a question there.

"Is that correct, ma'am?"

"Yes. It is. Look, let's go back to the conference room." I didn't want to alarm any clients who might come in, and I could tell that no one in the office would get any work done while he was there. Detective Davis followed me back to the little glass-walled room behind our desks. When I went by Lee, eyes wide, he mouthed, Want me to call Doug? I shook my head.

Once Detective Davis and I were inside, I closed the door behind us. He stretched long legs to the side of the table, ran a hand through his hair, and took a deep breath.

"Did you speak with Mrs. Miller?" He pulled a small notebook and pen from his jacket pocket. Just like on TV! I focused.

"No, I didn't. They said she wasn't available, that she was resting."

"They?"

"The personal assistant, Mr. Lewis, and a maid."

"Yes, ma'am. What time was this?"

"Late afternoon, four or four thirty, I guess."

"Yes, ma'am. And how long would you say you and Mr. Elliott were there?"

"It's hard to say. Maybe an hour, maybe a little longer. We waited for a while. Before we saw Mr. Lewis."

"Yes, ma'am. Did you talk to anyone else in the house?"

"Uh, no."

"And you and Mr. Elliott took certain paintings from the house?"

"Well, yes, but we were supposed to. Mrs. Miller said to."

"Mrs. Miller spoke to you?" The detective dropped his sleepy, disarming voice.

"No, I told you. They said she was resting."

"Did Mrs. Miller speak to Mr. Elliott?"

I started to answer, to begin all over again and explain the whole story. Then a childhood of lying on the living room floor watching *Perry Mason* flashed through my mind.

"Not while we were there at the house. I guess you'd better ask Mr. Elliott, though, right? Anything I said would just be hearsay, wouldn't it?"

Detective Davis laughed. "We're not in court, ma'am, just trying to understand what happened." The laid-back, folksy tone was back. Its reappearance made me feel suspicious and defensive.

"My understanding, and Doug's, Mr. Elliott's, was that Mrs. Miller wanted the paintings returned to the gallery. The maid and the Lewis guy kept saying that."

"Were you and Mr. Elliott together the whole time you were on the property?"

"Yes."

"There was no time when you and Mr. Elliott were separated either in the house or on the grounds. You didn't wait in the car for a while? Neither of you went to a rest-room?"

"What are you implying?"

"Not a thing, ma'am. Just trying to get everything clear in my mind."

"We don't know anything about this." I could hear the indignation in my voice, and I hated myself for it. I recognized the intimidation techniques, but I had let him rattle me anyway. I'd hate going through this if I had anything to hide. Then I remembered. "Oh. There were a few minutes. Mr. Lewis showed Doug a painting in another room."

"How long would you say you were separated?"

"No time at all. I don't know. Five minutes? Ten? Fifteen at the most."

"And were you alone during that time?"

"No, the maid was there. Well, she was there, then she went to another part of the house."

"Yes, ma'am. You don't plan to be leaving town in the next few days, do you?"

"Why? I'm not a suspect, am I?"

"Suspect? No, ma'am. There's no reason to be looking for suspects. Not at this point, anyway. We're just trying to clear this up. Get it settled quickly. We may have some more questions. Just get in touch with us if you need to go out of town, please."

"Sure." I sighed. "Look, I might as well tell you. You'll probably find my fingerprints."

"On the murder weapon?"

"There was a murder weapon?"

"No, ma'am, not unless you've got something to tell us." I thought he was messing with me, but I couldn't tell for sure. No chuckle this time, just the same dry, calm voice, but there was a gleam in his eyes.

"No, on the door handle. I might have seen Hazel lying in bed. I might have looked into her room."

"Might? You don't know?"

"Well, not for sure." I could feel a blush rising up my neck, and I felt even more embarrassed over that. "I just had a fast impression of someone, an older woman, in bed. Then I shut the door and went back to the entrance." I explained where I had been, which turns I had taken from the entry hall.

"She didn't say anything? You didn't say anything?"

I shook my head. "No, no. I just opened the door and shut it as soon as I saw it was a bedroom.

"Did you know Mrs. Miller?"

"No! I just went along with Doug because it was Jake Miller's house, and my dad has always been a huge Jake Miller fan, used to sit around with his friends playing these old songs when I was a kid."

"Okay. We may have a few more questions. It might be a good idea if you stuck close to town for a while."

"I didn't do anything, honest. I know it was rude. I never dreamed that would be her bedroom."

"Yes, ma'am. I'm sure we'll be in touch."

He gave me a card with his phone number, a number I recognized as the Metro police department nonemergency line, his mobile number, and his home number. "Thanks for your time."

I didn't know what to think. I called Doug's office, but he was in a real-estate closing. So much for my one phone call.

Anna had clients at her desk, but they wanted to know what was going on, too, so I told them as well as Lee, Anna, and Martha everything the detective had said. Then we got back to work. Or they did. I tried, but I didn't get much done.

I fixed a salad for dinner while I watched the six o'clock news, flipping from channel to channel to try to hear everything about the investigation. The news was that there was no real news. No revelations. Autopsy results were not yet available. The police were questioning several people who might have some information. There was film of Jake's daughter, Jackie, now a very conservative anesthesiologist who insisted on being called Jacqueline, or Dr. Miller, hurrying past cameras, shielding her face with a big handbag.

My friend MaryNell called. "Are you watching the news?"

"Yes. They don't seem to know anything yet, though. A detective came by this afternoon."

"Did he read you your rights? Did he cuff you?"

"He just asked a few questions."

"Was it this guy?"

"I don't know. I can't tell." I thought Sam Davis was the police detective in the scene, but he wasn't facing the camera.

"Have you talked to Doug today?"

"No. I called him, but he was in a closing."

Silence. She didn't say anything, but her question hung there. *And he hasn't called you back yet?* MaryNell wasn't a Doug fan.

"Hey, I'm gonna go. I want to see this. I'll call you later."

It was Detective Davis, standing in a drizzling rain, his tie slightly askew, now facing the camera, eyes showing unmistakable signs of too many nights with too little sleep. He said the police were investigating all leads and that it was too early to make a statement.

My phone rang. "Campbell?"

"I'll call you back, Mom."

"Do you have a suspect?" "Was Hazel Miller murdered?" Disembodied voices attacked the investigator.

His smile was hard and tired. "I've just told you, Dan, it's too soon for me to make a statement on this case. We're working on it."

Mr. Morgan from next door came over with tomatoes. "These are probably goin' to be the last," he said. "Weatherman said we might have a freeze by the weekend. I think Mildred's going to make green-tomato pickles with the rest. You doin' okay?"

So I told Mr. Morgan about the visit to Hazel's house.

"You don't mean it! Yeah, these new young kids, all hat and no cattle. They don't make 'em like Jake Miller anymore."

I nodded. What was I going to say to sweet Mr. Morgan standing there with his hands full of vine-ripe tomatoes? *Yeah, you're right, what country music needs is more woman-izing alcoholics?*

"Last time I went to the Opry, half of 'em had long hair. It sounds like rock and roll now."

I thanked him and made a tomato sandwich, eating it over the sink, the tomato juice dripping with every bite.

Then I called my mom and told her all about the detective's visit.

"You went into the woman's bedroom? And her sick?" I knew my bad manners would be what got Mom's attention.

I put on pajamas and called MaryNell back.

"Okay," she said, "start from the beginning and tell me everything."

"I've told you everything."

"Oh, come on. One more time. You might have missed something."

So I went through it again.

"So Doug couldn't have done it." She sounded disappointed.

"MaryNell!"

"Okay, okay. Let me know what you hear next — and call me if you need bail."

The rain had picked up, and it pecked at

51

the windows all evening. I cleaned four kitchen cabinets out of frustration. Cleaning cabinets is not something I do often by choice. I usually maintain a live-and-let-live relationship with the clutter in my cabinets, closets, and drawers. Out of sight, out of mind. Then an occasional attack of cabin fever hits, and I throw things out with abandon. Every time I do, of course, there is something in the pile of debris I have discarded or taken to the church benevolence ministry that I desperately need within the week. I studied a misshapen colander and tried to imagine any circumstances in which I'd want that thing back.

Doug called just after the ten o'clock news went off. "Sorry. I was in a closing when you called the office today. I didn't get away until eight. Then I went to the Y and ran." And he wasn't in a rush to call me back. "Did you see the news?"

"Yeah. Not much to see, though. What do you think?" I asked. "Was it an accident? Can we beat this rap?"

Nothing. Doug wasn't a good audience for crime jokes or bad Jimmy Cagney impressions. Or for jokes generally. He tended to take questions seriously. I told him about the homicide detective's visit.

"It could have been an accident or natural

causes. The human liver can only take so much punishment. You did the right thing, Campbell. Always tell the truth when you answer their questions. I don't think you need to worry. What motive would you have for murdering Hazel Miller?"

"Suppose I'm Jake Miller's love child, and I want my rightful inheritance? Suppose she surprised me in the act of burgling her safe?"

"In that case, I suppose you're in real trouble. Want the name of a good criminal lawyer?"

"Thank you. I might have known you'd disappear at the first sign of trouble." There was an embarrassed silence.

We'd had the disappearing conversation before, and Doug knew how I felt about it. The first time or two it happened, I was determined to get through to him. I knew he liked being with me, and I liked him. There was chemistry. I was attractive enough, blond, green eyes, fit without being obsessed about it. I could list plenty of flaws, but I knew I was at least considered pretty.

I tried honesty. I went by his apartment; I wrote incredibly eloquent letters. I would make him see how he was hurting me, make him see what a fool he was to pass up a wonderful woman like me, make him tell me how he felt and why he was acting like this. That worked about as well as passing notes in seventh grade, and I finally learned to leave him alone. Eventually he'd get over whatever it was, and we'd be together again. I may not have learned much, but I do know that I can't make Doug Elliott do anything he doesn't want to. And he knows exactly what he's doing when he doesn't want to face me.

CHAPTER THREE

The next day I decided to see what I could find out on my own. Contrary to legend, not everyone in Nashville is an aspiring country-music star. I, for one, have never spent my days plugging songs or putting together a project of demo songs, and I can't claim to be up on the buzz on the Row. But everybody in Nashville knows somebody in the business. I knew Stick.

Stick Anderson is a percussion genius. We've been friends since high school. I even know his real name, but I won't tell. Stick and I are occasionally painfully honest with each other. That's probably what has made our friendship last. Everybody needs somebody they can count on to be honest with them. Sometimes.

I knew Stick was playing at the Last Fret that Friday night. Stick's in high demand as a studio musician and on most of the big-name sessions. Whenever there was a sure-fire hit, a CMA award shoo-in release on the charts, you could bet Stick Anderson's name would be in the credits.

He says he's living in the best of all possible worlds. He gets paid to play; he can dress however he wants to go to work; and he gets to stay at home in Nashville. Life on the road, even in a luxury coach, can be grueling. It breaks up families and makes musicians and singers lose touch with themselves. It's first-class homelessness. It's more comfortable than a shopping cart on lower Broad, but it can be just as destructive.

Stick is talented enough and hot enough to be able to avoid the road. But he always downplays his success.

"I'm a drummer, man, and this is a picker's town. It's easy to be in demand when there aren't many of you." There are plenty of drummers, of course, but very few percussionists like Stick. He creates his own sounds, even his own instruments sometimes, always experimenting, always looking for a new rhythm, a new effect. That night, between sets, he was telling me about a sound he had used in a session the night before.

"You'll love this song. It starts with this kind of deep *aaoom* sound. I don't know how to describe it, kind of a breathy gong. I made it up. I'll play it tonight."

"Who was the session for?"

"New girl. Amber Blue." I raised my eyebrows; Stick grinned. "Yeah, I know, probably not the name her mama gave her. But she's got a great voice. She's been doing a lot of demo work around town; people are starting to notice her. So she's doing this project — four songs, got a good range, kind of a bluesy style. It's good stuff. Sony's interested, and several smaller labels."

"Will she make it?"

Stick shrugged. "She's good, but it takes more than that. It takes luck and timing, the right guy being in the right mood when he hears her stuff. And a lot of the labels are scared right now. Business stuff, mergers and takeovers. Internet downloads. Who knows? And then what have you got to look forward to? Three hundred days a year on the road. Not for me." He shook his head. "What's happening with you? Still seeing the lawyer?"

"Off and on."

"Where did I go wrong with you?" He sounded more like a grieved parent than an old boyfriend. "You know what they say about ten thousand lawyers at the bottom of the sea?"

57

"Yeah, right, it's a start."

"They're ruining the music, Campbell."

"That's funny. You don't look like your artistic vision's been stifled — or like someone who's missed too many royalty payments. I suppose a lawyer checks up on that?"

"Well, sure. I've got my lawyer. Everybody in town's got a lawyer. And you gotta check with them, and they've gotta check with each other before anybody hits a lick."

"You poor thing."

"Yeah, well, you hang with that lawyer, you always wind up depressed and cryin'."

I couldn't argue with that, so I shut up.

The Last Fret is one of the places in Nashville where you can still hear real music. It's one of the classic listening parlors like the Bluebird Cafe on Hillsboro Road and the Exit/In on Elliston Place, which, as the name seems to imply, keeps coming and going. That's where you see the real talent — the session players, the writers, the singers who aren't on the magazine covers yet, or anymore. People who've been around town a while talk about a young Jimmy Buffett playing to a nearly empty house at the Exit/In in the early seventies because Elvis was doing one of his last comeback concerts in Murfreesboro. I heard

Nanci Griffith at the Bluebird one night when she was unknown, and she blew me away. The shows at the theaters out around the Opryland Hotel are fine, but if you've got company from out of town and you want them to see the real Nashville, you take them to the listening parlors. That's what Branson, Missouri, can't duplicate.

"What's that on the napkin?" I asked.

"It's a song I'm workin' on," Stick said.

"Tell me about it."

"I have this theory that there's, like, this quantity of love in the world, in the universe. And, like, whenever you do a loving thing for a person, you add to that quantity. Sort of a physics of metaphysics. And when you do an unloving thing — or even miss the chance to love — you diminish that quantity of love for everybody. Kind of like spray deodorant and the ozone layer."

"I like it, Stick. It's deep."

"Yeah. Now, if I can just put it to a beat they can line-dance to, it'll be a hit."

"Compromising your artistic vision?"

"Just paying the bills."

"I hear you. Is Gordy around tonight?"

Gordy Adams is the owner of the Last Fret. He'd been part of Nashville's music industry before it was a business, much less an industry. He had helped so many people get a start or make a comeback that he had become a legend. Every year the whole business — plus most of the politicians and more than a few Belle Meade socialites — turns out for his birthday. It's a huge street party on Sixteenth Avenue. He knows everybody who is anybody, or used to be, or might be with the right break.

"Yeah, he's here. I think he's in the kitchen makin' barbecue sauce."

"Yeah?"

"Yeah. He's gonna do a guest spot on some cooking show on TV. He's practicing."

"Do you think he'd mind if I asked him some questions?"

"I should have known you didn't come out just to hear the incredible sounds I create."

I smiled. "That, too. What do you think?"

"Sure. Go on back. Unless the sauce isn't going well, it'll be fine."

Gordy was intensely stirring a huge stockpot full of barbecue sauce while his cooks tried to work around him. The kitchen would begin to wind down soon, though, when all the orders for this break were served. After ten, the bar did a heavier business than the kitchen. I stayed out of the way until Gordy looked up and noticed me.

"Hey, hon. How you doin'? I think this

may be the best barbecue sauce I've ever made. Wanna try it?"

I'm sure Gordy Adams couldn't have told you my name, but he knew my face, knew he'd seen me around, knew I was somehow a friend of Stick's.

"Sure. Stick said you're going to cook on TV?"

"Yep. Pretty silly. An old geezer like me pretending to be some fancy-schmancy TV cook."

"I think it's great."

"Yeah, well, my wife thinks it's hilarious. And she's right. But given the right inspiration and enough time, not to mention a generous supply of Jack Daniels, I can brew a mean barbecue sauce — especially if the judges drink the Jack."

"It smells delicious." He passed a spoonful over to me. It *was* delicious. It reminded me of barbecue I had once in a converted garage in Memphis near the Lorraine Motel. There were picnic tables and a few plastic potted palms in what had once been the service bays, and though I could probably never find the place again, it had the finest barbecue I've ever tasted. "It's great, Gordy, really great."

"You think so? Maybe, maybe." He sighed

and set down his spoon. "What can I do for you?"

"I just wanted to talk to you a little about Jake Miller, or, rather, listen to you. You knew him, not just the stories about him."

"You writin' a book?" Too many exposés and inquiring minds over the years had made Gordy cautious.

"No, no book. Promise. I'm just curious. All the talk about Hazel and Jake."

"Yep. It seems to be sellin' a lot of newspapers."

"What was the real story?"

"Who ever knows what the real story is? Whether you're outside lookin' in or right in the middle of it, all you see is what you see. And I've always been a little near-sighted. You think there's a song in that? But anyway, Jake's drinkin' had destroyed his first two marriages, that plus bein' on the road all the time. Well, that plus all the women hangin' around. And the fact that Jake always did marry the wrong kind of women."

"What do you mean, the wrong kind of women?"

"I may not be politically correct, but I don't suppose I've ever been too correct about anything else, and it's too late to change now. But a picker who's on the road a lot needs a woman who's solid, one who's gonna stay home and make it a home to come back to. Otherwise, there ain't nothin' there, 'cause you're out there carousin', stayin' up all night, and if you come home and don't find a real home, something that reminds you of your mama's and goin' to church on Sunday, if you come back to a woman who don't cook and dresses just like the women on the road, well, you might as well be in one more hotel room. Maybe it's not fair, but that's the way Jake was. He kept marryin' flashy women who liked the limelight just as much as he did, so there was nobody at home. Nobody made it a home."

"Hazel was like that, too, I guess?"

"Well, you've seen Hazel Miller. She ain't changed. She's no different now — or wasn't before she died — than she was when Jake first met her. Except maybe she could afford a better class of sequins after Jake died."

"What kept them together?"

"Well, I suppose Hazel liked the standard of living, and Jake had the grace to die young. But I'm prob'ly not bein' fair. I can't imagine they'd be a happily married old couple now if Jake had lived, but there was somethin' between 'em. It was like electric-

ity when they were together, kind of excitin'
but dangerous, like you weren't sure which
way the sparks would fly, you know? And
people who weren't careful got themselves
singed."

"Sounds like the voice of experience."

"Not me. Hazel was never my style. But I
was around enough to see a few people get
used, wadded up, and thrown away. Hazel
and Jake didn't seem to care who they hurt.
It was like they thought everybody understood their rules. And the only rule that
counted was, in the end, nobody counted
but Jake and Hazel."

"What happened when Jake died?"

"Don't know if anybody knows for sure. I
don't. Jake was on the road. He'd been
playin' up in Louisville and was on the way
home. Somebody said Hazel had been in
the audience that night. Some said no, that's
why Jake was in such a hurry to leave. He
wanted to get home to Hazel. Some said it
wasn't Hazel they saw waitin' in his car, but
some new girl, a singer who'd sung backup
in some sessions. His lawyer's the last
person who talked to him, as far as anybody
knows, except for whoever might or might
not have been in the car with him. Someone
heard Jake call his lawyer from backstage
and tell him he had to see him the next day.

If he said why, the lawyer never told. Client privilege.

"Nobody ever admitted to bein' in the car with him or drivin' for him — not Hazel or any girl or anybody else, for that matter. You know he died of alcohol poisoning, don't you?"

"Yeah."

"The alcohol in his blood was point-five percent, too high for even Jake to have been conscious, much less drivin'. The car ran off the road, hit a tree somewhere around Horse Cave, Kentucky. Today, they'd test the car for fingerprints, all kinds of scientific stuff, find out how long he'd been dead, stuff like that, but back then it was different. And he might have been Jake Miller, but he was still just another country singer who got himself killed drivin' home drunk in the middle of the night. Who'd question it? That's the way it's supposed to happen."

"Do you think somebody else was in that car?"

Gordy shrugged. "There were only two beer bottles in that car. If Jake's blood-alcohol was what they said, I don't see how he could have driven from Louisville to Horse Cave. And if he was drinkin' as he drove, there should have been more bottles in the car — and I'd have thought it would have been somethin' stronger than beer. Two beer bottles? It was the middle of summer. Looks to me like two people, drivin' along, stoppin' for a beer on the way."

"So who do you think it was?"

"That's the question, ain't it? I guess only two people know for sure, and at least one of 'em's been dead for forty years."

"What about the lawyer? Who was the lawyer?"

"Franklin Polk."

"And the girl singer. Who was she? Do you know?"

"Not really, but I always figured it was Rosie Layne."

"Rosie Layne? I never heard her mentioned in connection with Jake."

"She just did the backup vocals for his last record, and I don't imagine that rumor about her maybe bein' in Louisville was too widely known. Besides, it was just after that that she hit it big. Record contract, overnight star, went gold. Her career was bigger than Jake's by then. Seems to me like Franklin Polk had something to do with her career, too, early on."

"Thanks, Gordy."

"Anytime. Hey, let me get a jar. Take some of this sauce home with you. Let me know how it cooks up when you put some meat with it. I've made a ton of this stuff. What am I gonna do with it?"

I waved to Stick and left the Last Fret with a quart of barbecue sauce and a lot to think about. Franklin Polk and Rosie Layne. Kitty Wells might have been the queen of country music, but Rosie Layne ruled the Nashville music industry. The producers and executives on the Row and in New York and L.A. make the decisions that make and break careers, but Rosie Layne is like the British royal family. Gracious, living in a mansion just a couple of doors from Minnie Pearl's old house and the governor's mansion, every inch the lady and well dressed except when she's in costume for now-rare performances. She's the one who waves to the fans and is kissed by politicians running for reelection. She's the symbol of traditional country music. It was hard to imagine Rosie Layne as a young groupie singer waiting for Jake Miller at the stage door.

And Franklin Polk. Franklin Polk had been a major contributor to Nashville's most important — or at least most visible — charities for years. He's been on several prominent boards and endowment committees. You name it, Franklin Polk is there: the Swan Ball, Children's Hospital fund-raising, the Performing Arts Center, the symphony. Looking benevolent and relaxed as only a financially secure retired man can, Franklin Polk is always quietly significant. And always elusive.

I had a vague perception that the dean of Nashville attorneys was somehow connected to James K. Polk, eleventh president of the United States and onetime Nashville resident. So many Nashville names can be traced back to the city's founders and early residents or at least to the gamblers and wheeler-dealers who climbed off the riverboats and stuck around long enough to acquire respectability.

I had never heard Franklin Polk's name associated with any of the ongoing squabbling over Jake Miller's estate, though. He must have dissociated himself from the situation long ago, or his name would have been mentioned in the papers now and then. Funny, in a way, because that constant wrangling by the heirs over the estate must have added up to a lot of billable hours for Nashville attorneys over the years. Every so often one of Jake's previous wives would sue or some would-be would show up in town claiming to be Jake's illegitimate child or grandchild. Jake's account must have been a lot more profitable for his attorneys after his death than before. I decided I'd have to call and ask Doug about this one.

The Loaded Spoon is a really good meat-and-three on the ground floor of an office building a few blocks from the courthouse. I had called Doug the night before, and we'd agreed to meet there for lunch. Doug was waiting at a table in the back when I arrived. He ate while I filled him in on what Gordy Adams had told me. When I slowed down, he looked up.

"Leave it alone, Campbell."

"How can I leave it alone? The police are calling me. You got me into this."

"I know." He looked so uncomfortable that I regretted saying that. "But it's not my fault you were snooping around the house. On the advice of your attorney, leave it alone, Campbell. Don't ask questions. Don't go around telling people you were there that day. Believe me, you don't want to get mixed up in something like this."

"I'll remember that the next time you ask me to go for an afternoon drive." I picked at my chicken salad. "I knew I should have gone to Aruba for the long weekend. Now, can you find out how Franklin Polk was involved with Jake Miller and his estate?"

"Campbell!" Doug rolled his eyes in

exasperation, and I realized that was the closest I had ever heard him come to actually yelling at me — or anyone. "You're not listening. Drop it. And I didn't ask you. You asked me. Begged me."

"Yeah, but it just seems that someone would have talked to Polk, asked him what Jake's plans were. Did Jake say, 'Gotta go. Hazel's waitin' in the car'? Or 'See ya later, Frankie. Got a babe out there gettin' impatient'?"

"Somebody asked Polk those questions years ago. Jake Miller drank himself to death forty years ago. No mystery. Just booze and a car. Next you'll be telling me Jake and Elvis were standing beside the man who fired the shot from the grassy knoll, and that's why he's with Marilyn and Jimmy Hoffa in the federal witness-protection plan."

"Cute. Really cute. So what have you found out?"

"I've found out you don't have enough to do."

"Do you mean to tell me you're not the least bit curious about this? You don't care about finding out what happened?"

I could see anger in the sudden stillness of his face. Doug and I rarely have confrontations. That's something neither of us is good at, and we both tend to avoid it. That's probably a major reason why our relationship has been stuck for so long. Neither of us has had the courage to say it's time to fish or cut bait.

Doug's lips thinned to a fine, straight line. No wonder he wins so many cases. I knew I wouldn't want to be on the other side of a courtroom from him. The other side of a plate of homemade chicken salad wasn't too comfortable as it was. His eyes narrowed, then relaxed as he laughed, a not entirely pleasant sound. I don't know if the change was because of something he'd seen in my eyes or in himself.

"Okay. You're right," he said. "I'm curious. Nobody's talking much, and that makes me even more curious. Usually, in a case like this, every lawyer and clerk passing through the courthouse has absolute, for-sure, inside information straight from their law-school classmate in the DA's office or their personal assistant's best friend who used to work in the Justice Center, whoever. This time, nobody's heard anything. So, I'm thinking, are they just not talking to me because they've heard I was there, or is nobody talking? And if not, why not? Who's suddenly turned off the spigot to stop the leaks, and how? And why? What's so important about this case? Isn't this just about an

71

old alcoholic dying in her sleep? I don't like it. What is somebody hiding?"

To make a speech that long, Doug had to be really upset. "I'm sorry," I said.

He looked embarrassed, his eyes focused on the ubiquitous sugar, salt, and pepper arrangement at the side of the table. "It's not your fault. As you pointed out, I got you into this."

I reached over and touched his hand. Doug's never been much of a public toucher, especially not here in a courthouse lunch crowd, so I half expected him to pull away. But he turned his hand over and held mine.

"I'm sorry." That was the first time Doug had ever apologized to me, actually said the words. He might do all sorts of things to make it up to me when he knew he had hurt me, but he had never said "I'm sorry" before. He still hadn't looked up. "I don't like being involved in this, and I wish I hadn't gotten you involved in it, too."

"It's okay." I realized that I was almost whispering. "It's okay. It's been like a game to me. I hadn't thought about how uncomfortable it is for you being involved in something like this, working around the judges and DAs."

I wanted to say more. I wanted to tell him

72

I cared about him, that I wanted to be part of his life, even the scary parts, that he didn't have to be able to solve every problem, handle everything. But I didn't. It was probably way too late for that. The silence stretched. The moment passed. I guess I was afraid that if I said too much he'd disappear, and I really didn't want him to disappear right then. But I did want to know more about what happened to Hazel.

CHAPTER FOUR

On a day like today, if I was thirteen,
I'd be battin' cleanup, scorin' runs for my
team.

— Jake Miller,
"I Just Want to Be Here with You"

A few days later I was delivering some cruise documents on West End near The Mockingbird Gallery. On an impulse I stopped in to see Doug's brother. A half-dozen birds, mostly starlings rather than the signature state bird, chattered around the birdhouse mounted on a post by the walk. It was elaborate, a small model of an ante-bellum mansion, with thistle and sunflower seeds scattered around the miniature porch. Droppings on the landscaping pebbles below detracted from the charming effect.

Kenneth was talking with a client in the front room. I waved, not wanting to inter-rupt him, and he nodded vaguely. As he continued with the client, I wandered around the place. The hot artists were displayed prominently; some of my favorites were in the smaller side rooms off the main display area.

The Mockingbird Gallery is in an old house, converted in the sixties when the street began to go commercial. The rooms are large and have twelve-foot ceilings. There's space to see the works well, room to back away and view from different angles.

Kenneth had taken out a few walls, added quality, well-balanced lighting, and painted everything in soft, pale neutrals. When the walls were bare, it was a bland, personality-less place, but Kenneth had excellent taste and an uncanny sense of the next big trend. The works came and went like traveling exhibitions. The gallery was a marvelous, magical place to be. I couldn't afford most of the artists Kenneth represented, but I had been coming here long before I met Doug, before I knew there was any connection, and I always left refreshed.

I was examining a new sculpture by one of my favorite artists when I heard the bell on the door as the client left. The artist's work was in bronze and, like her other figures, about eighteen to twenty-four inches high. There is a strength and power about this artist's work that I am always drawn to, her sculptures always of a woman caught in an active, dynamic pose. This one was of a woman climbing a rope, her dress flowing about her, the airy feel of fabric somehow caught in bronze, a dramatic contrast to the tension of the muscles in her arms and legs. At least, I thought she was climbing. She could have been hanging on at the end of her rope. A minute later Kenneth found me. "Nice, isn't it?"

"Yes, it's beautiful. Kenneth, I stopped by to look at those paintings Doug and I picked up at Hazel Miller's that day. Is that okay?"

"Of course." He looked surprised and quickly turned back to the sculpture. "I think her work is getting more complex as she matures."

Kenneth understood what made art marketable, the indescribable difference between what would sell and what would not. He also understood, in a way that has nothing to do with style or school or period, the alchemy that turned paint and clay and metal into art. He touched the sculpture tenderly.

"You're right. I love her work," I said.

"Really? It's yours."

I gasped.

"I've put you through so much grief with

this Hazel Miller business. Let this be my apology."

"Kenneth, I couldn't. It's m-much too expensive." I was stuttering now.

"Sure, you can. Wait here. I'll get a box and some packing stuff."

I stood there, my mouth hanging open. This was so out of character for Kenneth Elliott. Doug might have some intimacy problems, but he is good and truly generous. He lives much more modestly than he could, because he gives so much away, although not many people know that unless they're directly involved with one of the causes he donates to. Kenneth, on the other hand, is selfish and rarely gives anything away unless there's an angle in it for him, and never without getting public credit for it. Kenneth Elliott, who in all the years I had known him, had never offered me so much as a business card, much less a piece of art, was giving me a five-thousand-dollar sculpture by one of the most popular, read marketable, artists in his gallery. What was wrong with this picture?

By the time Kenneth had returned with a sturdy box and packing peanuts, I had remembered what prompted me to stop by.

"Kenneth, if you'll point me toward those

paintings, I'll find them. Are they on display?"

"Why?" His tone was sharp at first, then smooth and friendly again. "I'm not sure where they are, actually. Some of them are probably out. Why?" he asked again.

"No particular reason. I didn't pay that much attention to them the day we went to pick them up. It didn't seem that important. I was too busy taking in the wax statue of Jake and all the memorabilia."

"We'll look around when I get this done." He continued packing Styrofoam peanuts around the sculpture. "Have you seen the new Wingo pieces?"

"No, which room are they in?"

"The front one. You must have passed them. I was probably blocking them when you came in. We picked them up just this morning, and I've already sold two and have two clients in a bidding war for another. You'll have to take a look before they go. It's a real departure for her, I think. Very bold. Tell me what you think."

I wandered back to the front room. Kenneth was right. It was a new direction for the Nashville artist. Dramatic, vivid, and dominating, free but somehow very disciplined. I liked them. I liked them a lot. I looked around a bit then went back to the room where Kenneth was taping up the box. He glanced up. "What do you think?"

"You're right. It's a new direction. A couple of them are so large, though. Not everyone would have a place that would be right for them."

"True, but in the right space . . ." He trailed off. "There." He taped the flaps. "All set." He looked up and smiled. "You'll find the right space for this, I'm sure."

I smiled. I wasn't quite sure what to say to this new Kenneth.

"I'll carry this to your car, but can you get the door for me?"

"Sure." I went ahead of him out the door, holding it as he negotiated the opening and the steps with the box. Then I ran ahead to the Spider and opened the door.

Kenneth braced the box in the passenger seat so it wouldn't shift and shut the door. "You shouldn't have any trouble. But do be a little careful about sudden stops."

"I will. Of course. And thank you again."

"My pleasure. See you soon. We'll have to get you and Doug to come over for dinner. Carey and I were talking about that just the other day. Let's do it."

"Sure. I'd love to."

As I pulled away, I tried to understand Kenneth's behavior. Maybe his investment

79

in the sculpture was a lot less than the asking price. Maybe he really did feel guilty about all the trouble he had caused. I couldn't wait to tell Doug.

The early twilight of late fall had deepened to full darkness while I was in the gallery, and I drove home carefully in the old 1966 Alfa Romeo Spider, bright red, that my dad bought used when I was a sophomore in college. He believed that when something was engineered well and built well it would last forever, if you took decent care of it. When I go home, Dad always changes the Spider's oil and drives it around the block to listen to the engine. I've taken it to the same mechanic here in Nashville for years, and when Dad's in town, he'll take the car over for service but mostly so he can talk with the guy. As the years go by, the Spider and I get more and more stares in traffic, and it gets harder and harder to find parts, but she hums contentedly and has never let me down. People always ask me if the maintenance isn't expensive, but my standard reply is "not as expensive as a car payment." The Spider also has one thing that anything built in the last couple of decades lacks: personality.

I was halfway home before I realized that I had forgotten to look at the paintings.

■ ■ ■ ■

I called Doug later and told him about my visit to the gallery. "He gave you what?" Doug was astonished.

"I know. I don't get it. But I like it. You think he didn't mean it? You think I should give it back?"

"He gave it to you? Because you admired it?"

"As an apology, he said. For all the trouble he caused."

"That doesn't sound like my brother. Kenneth doesn't care what kind of trouble he causes anybody. Speaking of trouble, have you heard from the police any more?"

"No. You?"

"No," he said. "I guess they've written us off. With any luck, anyway. He just gave it to you?"

"Okay, it doesn't make sense. But he gave me the sculpture. I didn't steal it." I was getting defensive. "He packed it and carried it out to my car himself."

"He could have been an artist himself, you know."

"Kenneth?"

"He was really good. Studied in New York and Paris. He was good, but he wasn't . . .

wasn't great. He wouldn't have changed art, like Van Gogh or Picasso." Doug paused. "And he wouldn't have made the kind of money he has. He said once that painting, just doing it, wasn't enough for him. Said he wasn't going to starve painting decorating accessories for rich housewives with no taste. So he became a dealer and sells other people's work. He hasn't touched a brush in years."

"I didn't know. That he'd been an artist, I mean."

"I think sometimes he'd have become a different person if he'd stayed with it. Poorer, maybe, but I think I'd have liked him better. What were you doing at the gallery anyway?"

"I was passing by. I stopped in because I wanted to look at those paintings, the ones we picked up that day at Hazel Miller's."

"Why?"

"That's what Kenneth said. No reason, really. I was driving by and thought I'd stop. I didn't pay much attention to them the day we picked them up. After all the waiting, we were packing them up and getting out pretty fast. And the guy in the truck was yelling. With all that's happened, I just wanted to look at them."

"Did you get any revelations from them?"

"No, I didn't get to see them. At first, Kenneth was helping a client, then he started packing up the sculpture. Then I forgot."

"You forgot? Just be sure you get a bill of sale and a statement of provenance on the sculpture."

"You don't think he'd take it back, do you?"

"He took back Hazel's, didn't he?"

I didn't hear from Doug for several days, nor did I try to contact him. I was busy at work, planning a group sales meeting for an appliance-manufacturing company. Two hundred fifty sales reps, some with wives, husbands, or significant others, would converge in San Francisco in a month. I had been planning it for a year, but this was crunch time. Schedules had to be finalized, room reservations reconfirmed, air tickets issued, receptions and spouse trips planned, audiovisual equipment reserved. No telling how much of it would have to be changed at least once before the meeting. Believe it or not, I enjoy groups like this. I'm a problem-solver, and there's a puzzle-like quality to arranging group travel. I get the feeling of putting the last piece in the right place when I wrap one up, but at this stage it can be all-consuming.

Who am I kidding? I put the last piece into place, and then I get a call. Somebody forgot that his son is graduating on the day they're scheduled to go out. Can he go out a day later than the rest of the group? And if the airline allows that, can this other guy come back a day early? And somebody else needs to check some outsize or weirdly shaped but essential piece of equipment. And can we get three rooms at the group rate for people who are flying on frequent-flier miles? They're not on the airline list, and somebody forgot to mention them. And can everybody sit in an aisle seat at the front? I don't really breathe until three days after they get back. The first day back, they're tired. It's not until the second or third day that I get the calls about the problems. And by then it's usually too late to do anything that will satisfy the client, too late for a refund, for sure. They just need to complain. Job security, I remind myself.

By the weekend, I was ready to unwind, so I called Stick to see where he was playing.

"I'm at the Bluebird tomorrow night. Come."

"It's probably sold out." The Bluebird

Cafe is a small venue. For a name act, you have to call early in the week for reservations.

"Probably, but I can get you in."

"Thanks." There was gratitude in my voice until Stick continued.

"You can carry my equipment."

"Thanks a lot."

He ignored my sarcasm. "You're welcome. Meet me there at six. I'm playing both sets."

I spent Friday night being self-indulgent. I picked out two DVDs: *Philadelphia Story* and *High Society,* two of my favorites. I had been wanting to watch them back-to-back, sort of a double-feature, festival kind of thing. Katharine Hepburn, Jimmy Stewart, and Cary Grant brought different qualities to the story than Grace Kelly, Frank Sinatra, and Bing Crosby, but I like both treatments. Who could choose between Bing Crosby singing "True Love" and Katharine Hepburn talking about the yacht she and Cary Grant had spent their honeymoon on? "My, she was yar."

I had some leftover salmon in my refrigerator from dinner with MaryNell at J. Alexander's a few days before, so I cooked a salmon pasta dish, a garlic-and-onion cream sauce over penne, then took a long, hot bubble bath in my antique tub. I had found the tub one Saturday when I got lost in Wilson County, east of Nashville, and spotted it in a front yard with zinnias blooming in it. I stopped to ask for directions from the elderly lady pulling weeds in a wraparound apron just like one I remember my grandmother wearing. She told me how to get back to Lebanon Road and, when I asked, offered to take twenty dollars for the tub. I gave her twenty-five, felt guilty at that, and arranged to pick it up the next week. The inside just needed a good cleaning; the outside took two coats of red paint. It looked great against the white tile in the bathroom, and it fit me perfectly. I could lean back and just reach the water handles with my toes to add a little more hot water if needed. And think.

Think about Jake living out his songs. Think about a lonely old woman who had gone from the focus of the country-music galaxy to an expensive, solitary bedroom in a house she shared with a couple of employees. I wondered how often the angry kid in the driveway who was so insistent on his rights visited.

After the soak, I watched the movies and gave myself a pedicure. Red, to match the tub. There is something to be said for a

Friday night alone.

I spent most of Saturday raking leaves. The maples were dropping red and gold all over my yard. The leaves were beautiful, drifting across the grass, and they made cool swishing and crunching sounds when I walked through them. I knew, though, from experience, that if I left them there, bright and beautiful and crunchy, sooner or later we'd have a long, hard rain, and they would turn into a sodden, sticky brown mess. They'd be ugly and harder to rake. The other problem was that if I left them much longer, Mr. Morgan would rake them for me. Mr. Morgan's in his eighties, and each year it becomes harder for me to handle the guilt when I come home to find he's done something for me that I've put off. I saw him start in on his yard that morning, so I pulled on jeans and a sweatshirt and headed out to do my part.

"How're you doing, Mr. Morgan?"

He jumped slightly and turned. He didn't hear well and hadn't heard me crunching up toward him.

"Oh, hey there. I didn't see you. I guess I'm doin' all right for the shape I'm in. I thought I'd get a start on these leaves. We'll probably get some rain this week."

87

I nodded. "It's a gorgeous day today, though."

We raked in comfortable silence, gathering the leaves onto one of Mrs. Morgan's sheets on the grass. Then we'd each take a couple of corners and pull it to the back, behind our houses, and dump the leaves off the bluff. We watched them fall the first time or two, drifting in the sun, catching in the weeds and brush clinging to the limestone cliff along the way.

"Won't be long till we get some really cold weather now," he said, leaning on his rake. "Mildred thinks we ought to move to one of those new retirement places."

"Oh, Mr. Morgan . . ." I was genuinely distressed. I didn't want them to go anywhere — and not just because Mr. Morgan tended to fix anything that needed fixing almost before I noticed it. I liked the Morgans, and I didn't want them to get older, to need to live anywhere except this high-maintenance little house above the river. My parents would be upset, too. They liked the idea of the Morgans keeping an eye on me.

"We're not going to do anything in a hurry. I don't know. All those old people. Mildred would have people around to talk to, but I don't know. She thinks this place is too much for me to keep up."

And it was, of course. Mine was too much for me to keep up, and he had more than forty years on me.

"I tell her I'm not dead yet, though. They've got a cafeteria you can go to if you don't want to cook, but cafeteria food . . ." He shook his head. "We'll see."

I could help him more. I promised myself I would. But I knew that he'd end up showing me how to do anything that needed doing. Or that, as usual, I'd just come in from work and see that he'd done whatever needed doing at his house and at mine. And that Mildred would have left half a casserole in my refrigerator.

We finished the raking — it would all need to be redone next week as more leaves fell — and had lunch, tuna-salad sandwiches with fried green tomatoes on the side that Mildred insisted I share.

I recuperated by watching the UT football game on my couch, the soreness creeping into the muscles I hadn't used in way too long as the fall light faded.

CHAPTER FIVE

I rode my first train when I was thirteen;
I jumped on a freight and was gone,
And I've never looked back to see where
   I've been;
I'm just ridin' and singin' my songs.

                  — Jake Miller,
           "Last Lonesome Train"

Six o'clock Saturday night, I was shivering, waiting for Stick in the Bluebird parking lot. He finally pulled up in the old, beat-up blue van he drives to gigs. Once upon a time, it was the only vehicle he owned and all he could afford. Now he drives a Land Rover except when he's working and needs to transport the drums and things he uses to make percussion sounds. Stick says it's economic camouflage. He thinks potential thieves are less likely to expect a fortune in percussion instruments to be in anything that looks as bad as his van.

"Hey," he said as he climbed out. "You ready to work? You wanna grab this?" Stick handed me a small gong.

"Whatever I can do for the arts."

"Just carry that and don't sing."

I helped carry in the lighter pieces — chimes, bongos — while Stick and a Bluebird employee carried the heavier stuff.

The Bluebird has been a Nashville fixture since the seventies. Tucked incongruously into a row of upscale furniture and gift stores in the Green Hills area, with its faded sign, the place doesn't belong. Signs in front of neighboring businesses insist that parking is for their establishments only. I always wonder why they care if somebody parks in front of a closed furniture store.

Inside, it's small and dark, with tiny tables crowded around a small stage area. Sometimes, as tonight, the tables and chairs are arranged around a central open space. In a rear corner is a bar and, at the back, tiny restrooms. Kris Kristofferson once said "Excuse me" to me in the crush outside those restrooms. His eyes were gorgeous — sad and knowing, but gorgeous.

As musicians and Bluebird employees set up for the evening, I found a spot out of the way and listened while they tuned up.

Tonight was Writers in the Round. Writers aren't always great singers, but there's a raw, honest quality when a writer sings his own song in a small, quiet setting like this, an intimacy between the poet and the listener that the best-produced CD with all its clean sound can't touch. This is how I like music best. And apparently I'm not the only one. Nights like this, with writers set up in the middle of a room singing and playing their own songs, taking turns playing each other's, have become more and more popular in Nashville.

Stick and two guitar players took plain wooden chairs in the middle of the small room. Stick sang the song about love, the one he had told me about. There was a second's hush before the applause — that moment when the audience catches its collective breath. You know you've just heard something special. And the singer knows you've heard it. This was that kind of night. I knew it was special. I saw a producer I vaguely recognized take out his iPhone and make notes. My guess was he was looking for material for somebody's next album. Looked like a cut for Stick on this one.

During a break, Stick introduced me to the guitar players. One, Randy Dean, was single and seemed a little interested in me, I began to think. He and I talked during the breaks.

"Stick says you guys went to high school together."

"Yeah. I wanted to be in his band," I said. "I play a mean tambourine. I could have been a star. But Stick said I couldn't sing."

Randy smiled. "Ah, what does he know about music? He's a drummer."

I looked around to see if Stick had heard, but he was across the room talking to the producer I'd noted earlier. "Yeah, lucky he's had some guitar-pickers to keep him in work."

Randy laughed. "I'd better get back. It's almost time to start again. You want to have dinner sometime soon?"

"Yeah. That'd be nice."

"Okay. Great. I'll call you."

The dreaded words. *I'll call you.* But I like this, I thought. Eat your heart out, Doug. It was nice having someone paying attention, trying to impress me.

Randy had written two songs I recognized, one a recent top-ten single by last year's CMA Entertainer of the Year and the last song of the closing set. During that one, he looked across the room and into my eyes, and I found myself wanting to believe the lines of his lyrics. I turned away, a little

93

embarrassed by the intimacy I might have been imagining, and a little suspicious. How many girls had he sung that song to? It probably worked well with most women.

Just as I turned, I thought I glimpsed a face that was naggingly familiar, but I lost it in the crowd. I edged my chair around to get a better look, and that's when I saw the long black hair, the resentful eyes — it was the kid Doug and I had seen yelling outside Hazel Miller's house.

The song Randy was singing was a ballad, soft and syncopated, and I couldn't get up to go over to the boy without making a scene. I shifted back to see Randy looking quizzically in my direction before he turned his attention to the neck of his guitar. The last chord faded into applause and acknowledgments and the scraping of chairs as people stood and began to leave.

I tried to make my way around to the corner of the room where the boy stood talking to a couple of men. People kept blocking my way; then I'd lose sight of him. I kept saying "Excuse me" and pushing my way around couples, through conversations. I saw him move toward the exit, and reached him just as he was going out the door. "Excuse me." I put my hand out and reached past the last two people between us to touch his arm.

He turned toward me, habitually angry boredom already stamped on his young face. "I'm Campbell Hale," I began. "I saw you outside Hazel's —" I watched recognition click in his eyes, and he turned and was out the door before I could finish my sentence. I tried to follow him, but a tall man in a cowboy hat with his arm around a blonde in tight jeans had crowded into the doorway. I needed to talk to the boy, ask him what happened after I'd left Hazel's.

"Excuse me, excuse me," I kept saying, trying to push through, but by the time I got out the door, I could see him rounding the corner of the Porter Paint store several doors down.

I'm no track star. I knew I'd never catch him, and besides, I didn't feel too good about chasing an angry man in the dark behind buildings and through alleyways, even in Green Hills. I went back inside to see Stick and his friends packing up.

Randy was cool; he seemed a little annoyed that I had ignored the end of his song until I explained why. I told him I had seen the boy outside Hazel Miller's house, and I was curious to know who he was. Seeing him again in this setting, with so many music people, it occurred to me that I could find out. I described the boy. Then Stick said, "I'll bet that was Jay Miller."

"Jay Miller?"

"Yeah, he was here tonight. I didn't notice where he was when you were at the door, but he was here tonight."

"Jay Miller? Who is he?"

"He's Jake Miller's grandson," Stick explained. "You know, Jackie Miller's son, except Miller's not his real name, of course. He uses Miller as a stage name, does some rock versions of Jake's old songs. The way you described the guy sounds like him."

"Yeah, he was here," Randy added, "sitting right over there." He pointed to the area where I had first seen the boy. Disappointed as I was at missing him, at least now I knew his name.

"Tell me about him. Should I have heard anything he's done?"

"I don't know," Stick said. "He's more into the rock scene than country. He's always had a chip on his shoulder."

Randy added, "I think he played at River Stages this year."

"Yeah," Stick chimed in, "he has a band. They call themselves Alternative Music City. They did a couple of Dancing in the Districts this past summer."

Not too many years ago, Second Avenue

was a run-down row of warehouses and old building-supply businesses. Rents were relatively low, and some courageous entrepreneurs began to move into the area with interesting businesses. There was an architectural antiques shop where you could find the most wonderful stained-glass panels, usually from old churches. A few restaurants appeared, then an art gallery in a gutted and renovated warehouse. The area began to catch on, and promoters began to call it Market Street, recalling its days as a commercial center when pioneer Nashville depended on river traffic.

Now there's a Hard Rock in place of the hardware store that carried every obscure bolt or bit you might need. There used to be a huge faded mural of a painter on the wall of the hardware store, which smiled encouragingly over the roof of a liquor store where Broadway crosses Second Avenue. The liquor store is gone now, and so is the painter, replaced by a giant Les Paul Gibson guitar. The Les Paul is a fine guitar, but it was the instant history that bothered me, I suppose. The painter is gone, replaced by a guitar. It's classic, historic in its own way, but not the painter who'd been a Nashville landmark as long as I could remember. The merchants who made the street fashionable can't afford the rent anymore, and it's tough to find a place to park. I don't go down Second Avenue very often anymore. I miss the painter. I keep thinking I need to go to the Hard Rock. They have a sweater of Buddy Holly's and an entire James Brown suit on display. But there always seem to be too many tourists around. I did go to the Wildhorse Saloon one night when Kris Kristofferson was making a rare appearance. His music was as raw and real as ever, but it seemed out of place in that artificially rustic saloon with fake horses drinking at the bar.

Now they call the area The District. Dancing in the District is a weekly summertime event, with decent bands, usually rock rather than country, and not always local ones. If Jay Miller's played Dancing in the District, he must be pretty good — or at least he must have somebody good promoting him. And River Stages, Nashville's annual street festival, held most Junes during the first stiflingly hot week of the year, attracts Nashville's top performers. I had probably heard Alternative Music City play without realizing that Jake Miller's grandson was in the band.

I thought back to his encounter with George Lewis at the house. Just what rights

did Jay Miller think George Lewis was deny-
ing him?

Chapter Six

It took three calls before I got through to Doug.

"How can I look up a will?" I asked.

"Whose will?"

I really didn't want to answer that. "Jake Miller's."

"You never stop, do you? Is there anything I can do to get you to leave this alone?"

I didn't say anything. I didn't want to leave it alone. I wanted to know what happened to the sad, lonely woman in the bed, or I wanted to know that nothing had.

"I guess not," he answered himself. "Well, I have to be in court in the morning. If you can be there by eight forty-five, I'll show you what to do."

I had plenty of vacation time built up. I could take the morning off. "I'll be there. Thanks, Doug."

This time he didn't say anything.

I made sure I was early the next morning.

By eight thirty I was waiting with the pigeons on the steps outside the courthouse, struck once again by what a leveler this place was. There were lots of suits hurrying in, lawyers doing their jobs. Then there were the people whom the courts exist to serve arriving for nine o'clock dockets. There were power brokers and prosperous people, but there were also the poor and neat, the dirty and sloppy. I wondered if no one, not even their attorneys, had told them that the legal system is not entirely unbiased, and they'd make a better impression with new haircuts and clean clothes that covered a few tattoos.

It must be hard not to become cynical, working in that building every day. The stories you hear in there are not about heroism and kindness and generosity, but greed and lies, broken covenants, pain, violence, and selfishness.

It's not like the small town where I grew up, where the courthouse was the center of civic life, where old men gathered to whittle and talk on Saturday mornings. People renewed auto tags, registered deeds. Kids registered to vote for the first time; hopeful couples applied for marriage licenses. In Nashville, though, as in most large cities, government is more compartmentalized.

For voter registration and auto tags, you go to the old Howard School building or convenient new community offices; marriage licenses, the current Howard School. The courthouse is reserved for crimes, lawsuits, divorces, and probate.

Standing on the steps, I could barely make out the spire of a church on Broadway, peeking over the tops of buildings. What a great gulf, I thought, between here and there.

While I waited, I read the bronze plaque set into the courthouse wall between the huge Art Deco doors. It commemorated the thirty-fifth anniversary of the bombing of then Councilman Alexander Looby's home on April 19, 1960. Many people don't know about Nashville's role in the civil-rights movement in the sixties. Selma, Birmingham, Little Rock, and Oxford had more violence and got more media attention. But the bombing here was an important milestone, drawing a moral line that illuminated the issue and forced people to choose a side.

I had heard my parents and grandparents talk about those times. Most people had been more concerned about their own lives, paying bills, what to cook for dinner, than larger social issues. Which might be why it took so long to change things.

The plaque quoted Joshua 6:20: "When the trumpets sounded, the people shouted, and at the sound of the trumpet, when the people gave a loud shout, the wall collapsed; so every man charged straight in, and they took the city."

I saw Doug's black BMW pause at the entrance to the underground parking. Eight forty-two. By eight forty-five, he was walking up the steps toward me, his face unreadable. His lawyer face, I called it.

"Hi. Thanks for meeting me. I know you're busy."

"No problem." He didn't sound like there was no problem. He opened the door for me, then led me through the airport-like x-ray security equipment that clashed with the marble and brass lobby.

"It's on the right," he said as we took the corner. He pointed to the door marked PROBATE CLERK, ROOM 105, in gold letters. "You'll need the DOD."

I looked at him blankly. "DOD?"

Doug shook his head. "The date he died. If you have any problems, I'll be up on the fifth floor in the circuit court. I can help you when I'm through. I just don't know when that will be."

"Thanks."

He turned to go, then turned back. "Umm, if you have time to hang around . . . we could have lunch."

"Okay. I'll find you upstairs."

I opened the door and found myself facing a long counter, bored-looking women at desks scattered around the room. The woman at the desk nearest me checked to see if anyone else was going to get up and help me. No one made eye contact with her or me; everyone looked busy. She sighed, pushed herself up from her chair, and ambled over. Her head was tilted to one side, and her eyes dared me to complicate her day.

"I need to look up a will," I ventured.

"You need the date of death; then *you* can look it up in the index."

I had expected a computerized database. I looked over the counter to see that she was pointing toward shelves under the counter that held ancient-looking oversize ledger books. I knew the year Jake had died, but not the exact day. I had thought I could search by his name.

Embarrassed, I mumbled, "Okay. Thanks," and retreated. DOD.

I pulled out my phone and searched for

104

Jake Miller. It took a while. My reception wasn't great inside the stone walls, with who knows what kind of electronic stuff buzzing around.

Jake Miller died on July 4, 1969.

I went back to the probate clerk's counter armed with my own information. This time the clerk refused to look up and make eye contact, determined to outwait her coworkers. A young woman finished explaining something to a visitor and turned to me.

"What can I help you with?" It was a pleasant enough start.

"I need to look up a will."

"You know the date of death?"

I told her the date of Jake's death.

"Okay. You need to come around here" — she pointed to the waist-high gate as she knelt behind the counter — "and look in this index book." She pulled out a huge ledger as I opened the gate.

This was a revelation. I had never imagined the public would be allowed behind the counter, touching actual records.

She set the ledger, labeled with the year Jake died, on the counter in front of me.

"What you're looking for is the Petition to Probate. That's usually one of the first entries, and it should be soon after the date of death. Just look for the name in this column." She pointed. "Call me over if you have any questions. I'm Shana."

She went back to her desk, leaving me to feel a little better about the civil-service salaries my tax dollars were paying.

The index listed each case in the order in which it was heard by the probate judge. I started on July 4, the date of death, running my finger down the column. Each entry was handwritten and revealed the date of probate, the legal name, the docket number, and the attorney or agent of record.

I found what I was looking for on the third page I examined. August 23, 1969, Jacob Elijah Miller, docket number 436085, attorney of record: Franklin Polk.

I walked over to Shana's desk. "I'm not sure what the next step is." I gave her the information I had copied from the index ledger.

"Let's see," she said. "Okay, what I need is the docket number, 436085. Those records are stored downstairs. I'll be right back." In about fifteen minutes, she was back with several papers.

"Okay." She handed me a sheaf of photocopied pages. "This shows all the filings in the case." The page on top listed several dates with notes beside each. "These others are copies of the will itself and the subsequent petitions. That should be everything."

I thanked her, took the papers, and climbed the stairs to the circuit courtroom on the fifth floor. I slipped in and found a seat in the back row. Doug was at the front on a bench along the side wall, and I smiled when I caught his eye to let him know I was there.

I haven't spent a lot of time in courtrooms. I'd met Doug there a few times and even held a friend's hand during her divorce hearing. But the actual atmosphere in a courtroom has always amazed me. On *Perry Mason,* it was so solemn, all the energy and attention focused on the witness and the opposing attorneys unless Della or Paul interrupted with an important message that always changed the case. In real life, at least in my very limited experience, it's entirely different, both more boring and more fascinating. Things happen slowly, with lawyers asking witnesses to repeat information that seems obvious. The courtroom was like a three-ring circus. There was something to watch everywhere I looked.

The clerk was flirting with the bailiff. The court reporter looked simultaneously bored and focused. The waiting attorneys were talking quietly, planning golf dates, probably. The audience came and went; babies squirmed. Every type, every economic class. Through it all, the judge droned, rarely surprised out of his routine. What was there to excite him? He'd seen and heard it all.

I liked watching Doug work, though. He's always well prepared and thorough, has documentation for every contingency. "Judges don't want to waste their time listening to attorneys be impressive," I'd heard him say. So he prides himself on keeping his briefs brief, condensing everything to its essential elements, a thin file folder. "That way the judge won't feel his lunch or late-afternoon golf game is threatened." In his briefcase, though, I knew there were stacks of citations, precedents, and information, ready to be pulled out if the judge needed convincing.

I settled in to see what I could learn from the papers. The will had been drawn up by Franklin Polk less than a month before Jake died. Most of the estate was set up as a trust. Hazel inherited fifty thousand dollars outright, but everything else — publishing rights, royalties on recordings, licensing, proprietary rights to Jake Miller's name and anything associated with it — all went into a trust, even the house. Hazel had use of the house and income for her lifetime or until she remarried. In either of those cases, the remainder of the estate would be divided among Jake's children. That's the way it was worded — "any child of mine surviving." I knew of only one — Jacqueline. I'd have to ask Doug, but it appeared to me that Jacqueline would have the right to sell assets of the estate. Not Hazel.

The terms of the will might explain Hazel's loyalty to Jake's memory all these years. As long as she remained unmarried, she was potentially a very wealthy woman. I suspected her fifty thousand dollars was long gone. On the other hand, if the estate were cash poor, only Jacqueline could sell off the assets, and she could only do so after Hazel's death.

My next document was almost as interesting. It was a copy of a petition, brought by Hazel M. Miller, for the discharge of Franklin Polk as administrator of the estate of Jacob Elijah Miller. There was a copy of a final accounting by Polk and a judge's order, sealed for twenty-five years, dismissing a claim against the estate made by Ruth B. Laine. A claim for support for a child. Was there competition for Jacqueline's claim to her father's estate?

I met Doug in the hallway when he was through. Without talking we started down the stairs, and he nodded to acquaintances on the way out.

When we got to San Antonio Grill on Commerce, the waiter came over to take our drink orders.

"Iced tea, unsweet, lemon and lime," I said.

Doug looked at the waiter. "I'll have sweet tea, lemon."

I picked up my knife, wondering if I really could cut this tension with it.

"What'd you find?" Doug didn't want me poking around, but I was stubborn enough to pursue the case in spite of Doug's demand that I leave Hazel's death alone. Or maybe because of it. Either way, I needed his help in understanding the documents, and he was clearly curious enough to help.

Doug heard me out. "The dead hand."

I felt my eyes go wide. "The dead what?"

"The dead hand. Legal term for someone trying to control his estate — and his heirs — from beyond the grave."

"Oh," I said, enlightened. "The lifetime-use thing."

Doug nodded. "You can't control what happens with your estate forever. But one generation. Yeah."

"So Jake is still pulling the strings." I shivered at the image of a hand from the grave controlling his family. "It's Jake's fault!"

"What are you talking about?"

"Odds are, Hazel is dead because of that will of Jake's."

"You're being way too melodramatic," Doug said, a little stiffly, "but basically, you might be right. My guess is there wasn't much cash in the estate. I don't think Jake was a particularly rich man when he died, and fifty thousand doesn't go as far as it used to. He was popular, but he wasn't a legend until after he was gone. And country-record sales weren't the big money back then that they can be now. His records are still being sold, and everybody's recorded his songs, so there would always have been some income, but the one-time potential of selling publishing rights would be worth millions. There's no telling how much that could bring."

"That makes Jacqueline look like a suspect. She wanted to get her hands on those publishing rights."

"Campbell!"

I changed the subject. "You going to the game this weekend?" Doug was a Vanderbilt fan. He had gone to college and law school there.

"No, it's a road game. Ole Miss in Oxford.

I'd like to go, Saturday in the Grove, but I've got too much to do."

Southeastern Conference football was an easier topic.

"How do they look this year?" I asked.

Doug shook his head. "We've got some talent. That linebacker from Lipscomb High looks good. The quarterback's throwing well, but we need a bigger O-line. We might win some games if they'll give this coach time to build a program. He seems to be able to recruit."

We spent the rest of lunch analyzing the conference. Tennessee and Florida had the best recruit classes. Ole Miss had a Heisman prospect running back. Auburn was a wild card. Did A&M and Missouri really belong in the SEC?

Safe ground. Nothing about old country singers or frustrated artists.

After paying the check, Doug stood. "Go back to work, Campbell. Do your job. Go home. Someday, if it turns out there was a murder and if it turns out Jacqueline did it, you can tell all your friends that you had it figured out first. I'll attest to that."

As we walked back up the hill to the courthouse parking lot, I refused to be put off by his patronizing. "So why did Hazel petition to have Franklin Polk removed as administrator?"

"Who knows? Maybe she didn't like him. Maybe she was mad at him because of the trust and lifetime-use clause. That's not the kind of thing Jake is likely to have thought of on his own.

"No, you're right," Doug continued. "If I were Hazel, I'd want someone I thought was more on my side. She's lived pretty well, though. There must have been a lot of money over the years."

"But why couldn't she pay Kenneth for the paintings then?" I asked.

"Didn't," the lawyer corrected. "We don't know that she *couldn't.* Maybe she changed her mind. Decided she didn't want them."

"Okay, but why would Jacqueline be so desperate to get her hands on more money? She's a physician; she's very well-off."

"Apparently."

"You mean she's not?"

"I don't mean anything. I mean stop speculating. How would you like it if someone were digging into your past, suggesting that you had murdered your stepmother?"

"Stepmother?"

Doug looked stricken. I suppose the last thing he wanted was to give me any information that might fuel my speculation.

"Doug! Was Hazel not Jacqueline's

mother?"

He sighed. "No. Yes, legally, of course she was. I thought you knew about all that. You're more of a country-music fan than I am. They adopted her as a small child, although the rumor was that she was actually Jake's daughter."

"Jake's? By another woman?"

"Surely you've heard this."

"No! I've never heard anything about that!"

"The birth mother supposedly brought her to Jake. She wanted Jake to support the child. This was way before the DNA tests they can do today. The child might have resembled Jake, but how could you prove anything? Especially if you had kept your relationship secret — if it actually was something that could be called a relationship. Jake and Hazel didn't have any children. Story is, Jake told the woman he would raise her child, adopt her, make sure she never wanted for anything, but she could never ask for more, never contact them again, never reveal the story."

"And she agreed to that?"

"She didn't have any money, probably couldn't take care of the child. The child's real father, especially a country-music star like Jake, must have seemed better than anonymous adoptive parents. If there's anything to the story."

"So, Jay Miller?" I asked.

"Jay Miller?"

"Jacqueline's son. Calls himself Jay. He's a rock musician. Alternative."

"Alternative to what?" Doug asked.

"Alternative rock, alternative music. You're out of touch with the new generation, aren't you?"

"By choice. So what is alternative?"

"That's hard to define. A band starts out, doesn't quite fit a mold, but then they get hot, so I suppose that makes them mainstream, therefore, not alternative. I heard an alternative song in a Muzak-type arrangement in a department store the other day. If you're on Muzak, you're definitely not alternative."

"You listen to this stuff?"

"Yeah, sometimes."

"Okay." He looked dazed. "Well, I guess the alternative Jay Miller is the grandson by adoption of Jake Miller and most likely also his biological grandson." Doug had talked himself back to comfortable ground with legalese.

"But not Hazel's."

"Right. Well, not Hazel's biological grandson. Her grandson by adoption, certainly.

115

And in the eyes of the law, an adoptive child — or grandchild — has the same rights as a biological one."

"So, when he yelled, 'I've got rights' . . ."

"What are you talking about?" Doug said.

"At Hazel's house that afternoon. He was the boy in the truck with the earring and the attitude."

"How do you know that?" he asked.

"Hey, if you're going to be mad at me and not call, I have to find some other way to spend my time."

Later that day, as I drove home from work, traffic was bumper to bumper on 440. I passed the time trying to figure out how all my pieces of information fit together. There were too many mismatched edges no matter which way I turned the pieces.

I crawled I-40 east out to the Briley Parkway exit, passed the Wave Pool, Opry Mills, and the Opryland Hotel, which keeps growing and growing and growing. Every time I figure out a decent place to park for events there, they announce a new addition and put my parking place under glass.

I took the Opryland Hotel/Music Valley Drive exit, past the time-shares, all the way to the river, where the road ends and you have to turn either right or completely around. That's where I live, on the banks of the Cumberland River, eroding ever faster now, thanks, some people say, to the riverboats and water taxis.

The house is built out of the limestone that lines the Cumberland, grown out of the rock beneath it as if part of the cliff, and the mosses and lichens that grow around the small yard see no reason not to climb up the stone as well. If I didn't have so many windows, it might be dark and gloomy, but the windows bring in the sky and the river, which change with the seasons, weather, and hours. Sometimes I can sit on the flagstone patio staring at the muskrats playing on the opposite riverbank and shut out the rest of the world. I understood why Mr. Morgan didn't want to leave.

I went inside, dropped my files on the table and myself on the couch. My walls are all white, and the rooms are sparsely furnished. My friend MaryNell told me once that when my house is cleaned up it looks like a really great furnished time-share. I *think* she meant it as a compliment. Uncluttered? Tasteful? Or is it just impersonal, a house for someone a little too closed off, afraid to let too much of herself show?

I had found the perfect spot, though, for the bronze sculpture Kenneth Elliott had

117

given me. I had put it on a plant pedestal under a recessed spotlight and still hadn't tired of looking at it. Every time I passed by, I had to touch it, feel the strong lines. I wondered what kind of work Kenneth had done. Doug had said he painted, but oil, acrylic? What style? What would he be doing now if he'd kept painting? Would he still be stretching, learning, or would he have finally settled for decorative accessories?

I put the kettle on to make some hot tea, strong, sweet, with a lot of lemon, and took my glass outside to the patio. The crisp air felt good. The red geraniums were beginning to get a little leggy, but I couldn't bear to prune away what might be the last of my summer color. That's my problem with gardening, not ruthless enough.

The river was still, too cool now for water-skiers and too early in the evening for the water taxis and riverboat dinner cruises. It was my favorite time of day, just me and the muskrats and the river.

The leaves were off the dogwood by my patio, but it was full of red berries. A lone mockingbird fussed at me. Usually there were several, a whole family with great voices. Good gene pool, I guessed. They reminded me of a family from the church I attended as a child. Six children, all of them beautiful singers, the Morrises. I'd gotten to the point where I thought of my mocking-bird family as the Morrises. But today there was just one bird, left to tend the crops for winter. "The berries are all yours, buddy." He wasn't convinced. I sipped my tea and thought back to Hazel Miller.

Doug was right, of course. Hazel's death was none of my business. Anything I might figure out would make amusing dinner conversation, but it wouldn't make any difference. Doug was right about a lot of things, I supposed, and that was a bad sign. Whenever I start to think Doug's view of life is right, it's a sure sign of depression coming on. I went inside to take a long, hot bath and practice the reflexology massage I learned on my last cruise.

I lay in the hot water, half dozing and thinking about Jake Miller. He'd been dead for decades, but he was still controlling things. One thing was clear: Jake hadn't trusted Hazel to manage his estate. She must have been furious. That trust, set up to protect the estate from being dissipated in Hazel's lifetime, offered at least two people a pretty substantial motive for murder. Jacqueline would inherit. For Jay to inherit, Jacqueline would have to die, too. But maybe Jay could persuade his mother to sell some of the estate's assets. Maybe he had known for years that she planned to do so when Hazel died.

Who would know better than an anesthesiologist what amounts of different narcotic and depressive substances a human body could take and how they might interact?

And what about Jacqueline's biological mother? Did Jacqueline know who she was? Was she still alive? Did Jacqueline know? The biological mother could have found out the terms of Jake's will as easily as I had. She'd want to know that he'd kept his promise to provide for their child. But who was she? And how did Rosie Layne fit into all this? Did she want Hazel out of the way so her daughter could control Jake's assets, maybe even share them with her?

Jake Miller had died a long time ago, and the way she had abused her body, Hazel Miller couldn't have lived a lot longer than she had. What was the hurry? Who would kill a lonely old lady for money that wasn't really hers?

CHAPTER SEVEN

You say that you love me;
I know that it's true.
We've been through so much for so long.
You've been here beside me;
You've tried hard to save me;
You're the best friend that I've ever known
Except for this bottle right here.
— Jake Miller,
"The Best Friend That I've Ever Known"

The drive to work the next morning was breathtaking. It's true that morning rush-hour driving in Nashville often takes my breath away, but that morning it was because every tree seemed to have put on its most brilliant colors overnight. Leaves had already started falling, but the trees that turned colors hadn't changed until that evening. The maple beside the stop sign at the end of my street had turned a brilliant yellow gold, and when the sun shone through it just right, it glowed like a giant yellow lantern. Every stop sign should have such a tree beside it. It would go a long way toward eliminating road rage.

I didn't have much time for Jake Miller and his family and friends once I got to work. One of the agents in the office was having a crisis. A late-season tropical storm was threatening Puerto Rico, and she had clients booked on a Saturday cruise out of San Juan. The cruise line wasn't ready to cancel or even move the embarkation to another port. Tropical storms are unpredictable. In two days, San Juan might be in the clear, and the alternate port might be stormy. But the clients naturally wanted to know what was going to happen. Would their money be refunded? Were weather conditions going to be safe after all? They didn't want to spend all that money to fly into a dangerous area and be stuck there. We pulled up the Weather Channel Web site and followed the storm forecasts, just as the executives of the cruise line were likely doing. Everybody's best guess was that the storm was going to turn northeast. If that happened, San Juan and the cruise itinerary would be spared.

A call from a regular client, a huge University of Tennessee fan even though his daughter is on a full cheerleading scholarship at Alabama, reminded me that Bowl season was approaching. The Bowl Championship Series rankings had just been announced, and even though they weren't the final rankings, it was time to start looking for Orange Bowl packages. This year he might have two bowls to juggle.

By late afternoon, the tropical storm was stalled.

Doug called just before I left work.

"I really hate to say anything that might give you any more excuses to stick your nose where it doesn't belong, but I had a strange conversation today. I ran into Franklin Polk on the stairs in the courthouse."

"I thought he was retired."

"Very. I can't remember ever having seen him in a courtroom."

"What was he doing there?"

"I don't know. He could have been there to help out some friend who doesn't trust the young whippersnappers who run his office these days."

"Whippersnappers?"

"Everything's relative. I had the impression that he was waiting for me. And I didn't think he even knew me. Called me 'son,' patted me on the back. Said he'd heard my 'lady friend' had gotten 'mixed up' in 'this Hazel Miller mess.' "

"Do men have lady friends anymore?"

"If we do, our lady friends don't go around trying to make trouble. They bake; they garden; they play golf; they can even work if they want to, but they know their places. They look good and don't talk much."

I couldn't help myself. "Maybe that's why men don't have lady friends anymore," I offered sweetly.

"Anyway, he said he'd heard good things about me, heard I had 'what it takes,' even heard my name mentioned for state legislature. He said he'd been wanting to get to know me, said he takes an interest in the 'rising lights of the new generation.' Said he'd hate to see such a 'promising career,' a young man with such 'potential' 'stained' by such an unnecessary and unproductive 'situation.' "

"So am I a lady friend or a situation?"

"Either way, you're trouble. And hard to get rid of, like coffee on a white cotton shirt."

I managed to avoid a violent response. "Thank you. So what does this mean?"

"It means something is important enough to get Franklin Polk out of Belle Meade and downtown climbing stairs. It means somebody besides me wants you to leave this alone."

"I don't understand. Exactly what am I doing?"

"You're asking questions. You're stirring the pot. You're making mountains out of a molehill. You're airing a lot of people's dirty laundry. What is it you don't understand? You're upsetting somebody. And it's none of your business."

I could tell I was upsetting Doug. I wasn't sure whether he was more worried about my safety or his career.

On Wednesday night, with the tropical storm named and upgraded to a Category 2 hurricane, a friend who works for *The Tennessean,* the only daily newspaper in town since the *Nashville Banner* closed, called me at about midnight.

"I thought you'd want to know about this," Mark said without preamble. "Jake Miller's wife was murdered. It'll be in tomorrow's paper."

I had been asleep for about an hour, so it took a minute or two for my brain synapses to switch back to awake. There were remnants of a dream. Something involving Sean Connery in a kilt. "She was murdered? Who did it?"

"They don't know yet, or at least they're not saying. But the story is that she was drunk and drugged, and they think somebody got impatient and held a pillow over her face."

"Talk about overkill."

"Yeah. Official cause of death is asphyxiation."

"How can they tell it was murder?" I asked. "Everybody knows she drank a lot. It's not that uncommon for someone to take something that can be fatal with alcohol in your system."

"It seems that she did not have a prescription for one of the sleeping medications in her system, and there wasn't a bottle for it in her room either. Where did she get it? It's enough to make them pursue it as homicide. Besides that, one of the medications is especially dangerous with alcohol. Plus something about the color of the lungs tells them the cause of death was actually asphyxiation."

Mark was a researcher, a relic of the days when Nashville's two newspapers competed for news, when *The Tennessean* was an independent newspaper — a "real paper," as the old-timers say — that broke important stories regardless of which advertiser might be offended. It's amazing that Mark's hung on. So much of what's in the paper these days is canned, not written locally anymore. Except for local news, you can read the same stories in any paper owned by the same publishing chain. It's more cost-efficient. There are a lot fewer reporters than there used to be, but Mark is one of those people who knows everyone and can do anything, so I suppose they can't let him go even though they don't publish as many investigative pieces anymore.

"Do you know what the medication was? And what her blood-alcohol level was?" I asked.

"Nope," Mark said. "The guy on the police beat told me this as he came in to work. He was in a hurry to write it and get it on the wire. This is big enough that they stopped the presses to change the front page for the city edition. It's been a long time since I've seen that happen. I'll try to talk to him when he's through. I could pull his story up on my terminal, but he's bound to know more than he can put in it — who said what off the record, who raised his eyebrow when, nuance stuff. Want me to call you back tonight or wait until morning? It could be late."

"When's the last time you looked at a clock? It's already late. Yeah, call me back. I want to know what's going on."

"Okay. Sleep tight."

"You're kidding, right?"

Mark called back an hour later. "Good morning." Way too cheerful.

"Right. Have a nice day. What do you know?" Grogginess and sleep deprivation overcame courtesy. I hadn't been able to find Sean again.

"The official statement from the lead homicide detective is that 'it's an ongoing investigation, and the department is pursuing all leads. It appears that Mrs. Miller did not die of natural causes, but I have no further comment at this time.' "

"Any suspects?" I asked.

"No comment except that it's too early in the investigation to discuss that at this point. However, 'highly placed sources, who refused to be identified' — in other words, the police-beat guy's cousin who's on the force — 'said that unusually large quantities of at least two prescription medications, in addition to alcohol, were found in Mrs. Miller's blood and stomach contents. Police were questioning Mrs. Miller's household staff and family again.' "

"Hmmm. Anything else? What about the nuance stuff?"

"The personal assistant, what's his name,

Lewis, is their odds-on favorite. The house-keeper could have done it easily, but they don't figure she'd have enough to gain, and she doesn't strike them as a coconspirator."

"What about the daughter? Jackie?" I asked.

"On the surface, she'd seem to have the most to gain and she is an anesthesiologist, so she'd know what it would take to make sure someone wouldn't wake up, but they haven't been able to place her at the scene."

"Anybody mention her son, Jay Miller? At least, that's his stage name," I said.

"Not as a suspect. Why?" I had Mark's attention.

"He was there that afternoon, maybe not inside the house, but I saw him in the drive, yelling." I told Mark the story. "He certainly wanted in."

"Okay, I'll pass it along. I suppose if you've told the police this, though, they've already checked it out."

"I don't think I told the police."

"Campbell?"

"I answered their questions. They didn't ask me about anything outside the house. They just asked me about where I had been and whom I had seen inside."

"Didn't it occur to you that this might be important?" Sarcasm tinged Mark's voice.

"I didn't know she was murdered until an hour ago. I just knew they found her dead right after I was there. And I didn't know who the kid was when the police called."

"Look, this is going to smell no matter how you do it, but I think you should call the police investigator you talked to and tell him what you know. I'll wait until tomorrow, then tell the guy here. We've already gone to press a second time anyway. They wouldn't stop it again. That'll give you some time to tell the police before they hear it somewhere else and wonder why you're holding back."

It's hard to think clearly at one in the morning. "You're probably right. Listen, Mark, don't tell your guy until you've talked to me, okay? I want to talk to somebody before I call the police."

"Who?"

"Jay Miller."

"Campbell, I love you dearly, but you're an idiot. He could be the murderer."

"I don't think so. I just want to talk to him. I won't go off alone with him. I'll do it in a safe place. Promise."

"There's no such thing. Why are you doing this?"

"I just want to talk to him before the police do. I won't have a chance after that."

And, I thought, he'll be much more guarded, even talking to me, once he thinks the police may consider him a suspect.

"Don't be stupid."

"Don't be patronizing."

"It's not patronizing to want to keep you from getting yourself killed."

"I'll call you." I hung up before he could finish the sermon.

I decided one thirty in the morning was too late to start looking for Jay Miller, so I tried to go back to sleep. When I finally did, I kept dreaming of suffocating and pillows over my face.

The next day I checked the phone book. No J. Miller that looked promising. There was an office listing for Jacqueline Miller, MD, but I wasn't ready to try that route.

I called Stick. "I don't know, Campbell," he said. "No idea. I can check around and see if he's playing anywhere. I don't know him well, so I don't know where he lives or who his friends are. I'll ask around. Why do you want to find him?"

I didn't think Stick would be any more encouraging about my detecting efforts than Mark had been, so I gave him an edited, maybe slightly fictionalized version.

"I wanted to talk to him about his grandmother and grandfather, I guess because of having been there the day she died, seeing the memorabilia and all. My dad has always been such a fan, you know." It sounded weak, even to me.

"You're going to poke around in this some more, aren't you?"

"Poking around sounds awfully, I don't know, nosy, undignified. I'm just interested."

"Yeah, right. I probably shouldn't, but I'll ask around and let you know what I find out."

"Thanks, Stick. Your friend Randy seemed nice. Talented guy."

"Yeah. I think he was impressed by you, at least until you ran out in the middle of his set, during his hit even. That never happens to him. Come hear us Friday night. We're at the Bluebird again."

"I'll do that."

I read the newspaper with a pleasant sense of déjà vu, already knowing what the story would say, and made my next call to Doug. "Have you seen *The Tennessean* this morning? They're calling Hazel's death a murder."

"Hi, Campbell. Yeah, I saw it. Is this your one phone call, or haven't they caught you yet?"

"That's good, Doug. You're making jokes.

132

I like that."

"That wasn't joking. That was sarcasm."

"Oops, sorry. My mistake," I said. "I keep trying to give you credit for a sense of humor." I really didn't want to keep annoying Doug. Why did I?

"Did you call just to insult me?"

"No, I didn't call to insult you. Don't you think it changes things since the police have decided Hazel was murdered?"

"What do you mean?"

"I mean we didn't tell them everything. The boy in the driveway!"

"Did you answer all their questions?"

"Ye-ee-ss. Except for the boy . . ."

"Did you answer all their questions truthfully?"

"Ye-ee-ss. You know I did, except . . ."

"Did you answer all their questions, as they asked them, truthfully?"

"Yes."

"Then you've done your duty as a law-abiding citizen. Anything else is meddling. Why do you want to get some poor kid in trouble? It seems to me he's had trouble enough just being born into that family. Leave it alone."

I didn't think my relationship with Doug was improving.

I hung up the phone and went back to

work. The hurricane had turned northeast after all, heading away from San Juan. I moved on to the coach tour of Midwestern art museums I was planning for next April. The brochures were overdue at the printer, and I wasn't finished yet. The Kansas City hotel and I were having trouble agreeing on a price. One dinner in Chicago had fallen through and would have to be replaced. I was thinking of Pizzeria Uno, a classic in Chicago and my personal favorite, but the clients were likely to be retirement age. Would they want pizza, even really good pizza? Would most of its menu be forbidden to clients on high-blood-pressure medicine and low-sodium diets? Was it patronizing to assume they wouldn't enjoy pizza? I called to request a menu and group pricing and decided to call my mom later for her opinion.

While I was on hold, waiting for the restaurant manager, I thumbed through the catalog and newsletter from one of the museums on the tour. It was a smaller museum, but it had some very notable works, thanks to a cattle-baron benefactor, and its location was desirable — St. Louis. Next April, that particular museum, the Smith Logan Art Museum, would be featuring a traveling exhibit of minor (less well known, not bad artists) late-Impressionist French painters. That was ideal. Nonthreatening. Real art, but also pretty. My clients would buy lots of reproduction note cards in the museum gift shop, printed tote bags and umbrellas, and everyone would be happy.

On the phone, I could hear dishes and flatware rattling and the distant sound of two men arguing. I turned back a page in the catalog. A painting in the exhibit reminded me of one of the paintings Doug and I had taken from Hazel Miller's house. Of course, I'd only seen it for a few minutes, and one Impressionist floral study can look very much like another. Still, there was an element that was familiar, something I liked about the play of colors and light. Maybe the same artist? The manager finally got on the line, and I was off solving problems and planning for the tour's unforeseen circumstances.

I decided Doug's brother, Kenneth, would be the natural person to ask for advice about the galleries and museums I was considering. We seemed to be best friends these days. I placed copies of brochures from my top choices in an envelope and addressed it to Kenneth at The Mockingbird Gallery. I included a note: *What do you think? Are these worth it?*

While I was wondering what to do next, the detective, Sam Davis, called. "I'm sorry to bother you, Miss Hale, but we need you to drop by the station." He sounded as if he were asking me to drop in for coffee. "Since you were in Mrs. Miller's bedroom, we need to eliminate your fingerprints. Seems they're not on file."

"No, they wouldn't be. This is my first time as a murder suspect."

He laughed. It was a nice sound. "Yes, ma'am," he said. Yes, ma'am! Was he serious? Did he really think I could have killed Hazel Miller? "We just need to eliminate the prints of people we know had a reason to be there" — he paused, and I was sure I heard a trace of amusement then — "more or less."

"Does it matter when I come?"

"Anytime today will be fine. We appreciate your help." His good-cop, your-policeman-is-your-pal routine was getting a little tiresome. "And I'd like to ask you a few more questions about what you saw that day, if you don't mind."

Instead of having a bacon, lettuce, tomato, and avocado sandwich at The Food Company, I drove through Krispy Kreme and spent my lunch hour downtown having my fingerprints recorded.

Behind a glass barrier, a receptionist in a too-tight police blouse with a name tag that read MARIE raised an eyebrow. "Hep ya?"

I asked for Detective Davis. As I waited, uniformed officers came and went, talking and laughing, flirting with Marie, the door beside the barrier setting off a buzzer each time it opened. I wondered if they had an office pool on how far that button on her blouse would fly when it burst loose.

Finally Detective Davis opened the locked door. He was tall, very tall, and looked like he might be attractive if he weren't so tired. I'd like to see him unstressed; so far, I'd only seen him in the middle of a murder case. "Miss Hale?" He offered his hand. I shook it, a strong and solid handshake, and felt inexplicably embarrassed.

"Yes."

"Thanks for coming in." He nodded to Marie, and I followed him down a narrow hall. The walls were lined with notices and safety reminders. He entered into a tiny office and he motioned me to a wooden chair.

"Would you like some coffee, a Coke?"

"A Coke, thanks." My mouth was suddenly dry.

He left and returned with two Cokes in cans. He sat down behind a desk stacked with papers and files, leaned back in his chair, rubbed his eyes, and took a deep breath. He pulled a form on his desk closer and peered at it. "Miss Hale. Campbell. Unusual name." He looked up, a question in his eyes.

I figured it was my turn. "I guess." Had he forgotten that we had already met? That he had sat in my office and disrupted an entire day's work?

He nodded and took another deep breath. "So you were in Hazel Miller's bedroom the afternoon she was killed."

I started. Then I stuttered. "Well, I, not, I mean . . ." I stopped and took my own deep breath. "I guess. I don't know. Maybe. I was in the house; I walked down a hallway . . ." I closed my eyes, trying to see it again. "I was in the entrance hall; then I went to the right, through a sitting room, parlor kind of place. Then the dining room. Okay, the hallway went off to the left. Yeah, then the door was at the end of the hall." I nodded. "I only opened one door, you know. It wasn't like I was going around opening every door I saw," I explained, suddenly defensive.

Detective Davis nodded, watching. "What did you see exactly?"

"In the room, you mean?"

He nodded. "Or on the way, in the dining room, in the hallway? Any other people?"

I shook my head and thought. "No other people, definitely. Nothing in the hallway, nothing to notice. I didn't see anybody else. Nothing out of the ordinary."

"And when you opened the door?" he prompted.

I looked away, trying to concentrate on the memory. "The room was very dim. I had an impression of lots of chintzy fabric, you know, ruffles, florals, bed skirt, drapes, and curtains. Like it had been done expensively, but not recently. It seemed too still, but maybe that's because I was scared." I looked back at the detective and shrugged. "Maybe because I knew I wasn't supposed to be there and didn't want to disturb her. I just knew I wanted to get out of there as fast as I could." I stopped, but he didn't speak; he waited. "I don't know. Maybe I'm remembering something that wasn't there, but it was still, too still, and stale. But I think a curtain moved on the other side of the room. I don't know if I mentioned that before, but I've been thinking about it ever since I heard that Hazel died. I was in such a hurry to back out of the room at the time." Did I see more than I realized? I concentrated, but that was all I could come up with. "I don't know."

"Can you draw it for me?"

"Draw it?"

"Sure," he said, pushing a yellow legal pad and a pen across his desk. "Just a sketch. I'm not an art critic."

I eyed him.

He smiled and shrugged. "Just give it a try."

I took the pad and pen. I sketched the bed with a small lump where a head might rest on a pillow, ruffles on the bed skirt, a round table, I think, on the near side of the bed. Was there a phone there?

Beyond the bed, a wall of windows, long windows, French doors, maybe? The rest of the room, to my left as I stood at the door, was dark, shadowed. I hadn't looked in that direction. But the windows. There were liners, pulled shut, that dimmed the light, with drapes swagged back, and it was there behind the thicker, solid drapes, that something wasn't right. Had it moved? It couldn't have been the wind, and the air was too still for it to have been central air-conditioning. Was there a bulge? Had someone been standing there, slipping behind a drape as I opened the door? I don't know.

I looked up. "That's the best I can do."

He picked up my sketch and studied it.

"Well, you were in Hazel's bedroom, all right." He nodded to himself. "There are French doors that open to the back of the house, but they weren't open, not when I got there, at least, and air-conditioning wouldn't have moved those heavy drapes. Lewis called us when he found her dead. Or he called nine-one-one. The first responders wouldn't have opened the doors. I have their report detailing everything they did on the call. I've stood in the room while the air-conditioning came on and off. Could there have been somebody standing behind the drapes?"

"I don't know." I wanted to remember seeing someone there. I was beginning to understand why witnesses were so unreliable.

He smiled. "I guess this makes you either the last person to see Hazel alive or the first one who saw the body. Let's get you down to Fingerprint."

If his purpose had been to get more information, I couldn't see how anything I had told him would help. If his purpose had been to scare me, then he had been incredibly successful. I held my hands together as I followed him down the hall.

He stopped in front of a door near the front desk. A camera ominously faced a scaled background on the opposite wall.

"Well, Miss Hale" — he smiled — "I'm sure I'll be in touch." That sinking feeling in my stomach told me I was sure he would, too. He started back toward his office, then stopped and pulled a card out of his pocket to hand me. "You'll call me if you remember anything else, right?"

I nodded and tried to smile.

Inside the room, Marie with badly over-bleached hair and the too-tight uniform didn't seem to think I was a dangerous suspect. She seemed bored as she aligned my fingers on a glass surface attached to a computer monitor. "Right, roll it. We want a nice, clean print. Hey, Gary, you doin' all right?" She brightened when a young uni-formed policeman walked in. My finger-prints appeared in green swirls and red dots on the screen.

"Not as right as I could be," he leered.

"Now, Gary, you askin' me out or just sexually harassin'?"

"You decide, Marie. Your call."

I had the impression Gary and Marie had this conversation often.

"You got some residue on your fingers," Marie accused. She tore open a small packet and wiped my fingertips with an alcohol swab. Krispy Kreme residue. Marie started over and got through with me quickly.

Now The Man had my prints. I didn't like it.

Chapter Eight

On my way home that afternoon I drove by Hazel Miller's house. It wasn't exactly on my way, and I was sure neither Detective Davis nor Doug would approve, but I was curious. I slowed the Spider, and its old engine almost stalled. Time for a tune-up. Maybe it was time to rebuild the carburetor. Vans from two local television stations were parked in front of the estate's locked gates. One reporter was talking while his cameraman filmed, small satellite dishes feeding the footage to the networks. It wouldn't be big news nationally, but it would add a minute or two of human interest between international crises.

On an impulse, I took the next right, heading west off Franklin Road, then turned right again so that I was behind the Miller estate. A lot of these places have alleys behind them. When I thought I'd gone far enough, I turned up a small, unmarked gravel drive. Thick hedge and trees lined it, so I couldn't see anything until I rounded a sharp curve and found myself at a small, white guardhouse. The gate was unlocked and standing open; the guardhouse was unoccupied. I stopped and idled the car for a minute or two.

Nothing happened. I couldn't see anyone or any movement. Slowly, I drove through the opening.

I was at the back of a long lawn. I followed the drive to a large garage, designed to hold six cars. Two overhead doors were open. The drive continued around the house, presumably to the front where Doug and I had parked.

I had stopped the car and stepped out onto the drive before I saw anyone. Hazel's personal assistant, George Lewis, approached from the nearest garage door. A thin glaze of politeness covered the anger in his face.

"You'll have to leave. This is private property, and you're trespassing. If you don't leave immediately, I *will* call the police." He sounded as if he'd given this speech more than once today. Just then he recognized me.

"Oh, Miss Hale, right? Sorry. There've been so many reporters and busybodies today. Is there something you need?"

What could I say? I was just a busybody, myself. "I heard the police have decided Mrs. Miller's death wasn't an accident," I said.

"Not an accident," Lewis repeated. "That's a very diplomatic way to describe murder to a suspect."

"I suppose I could be one myself. But what could *you* have had to gain?" Unless, of course, Lewis was being paid by someone else, someone who did have something to gain from Hazel's death. "You had a good job, couldn't have been too hard."

"Exactly. That's what I told them. I had everything to lose and nothing to gain from Hazel's death." Lewis was wearing jeans and a work shirt and peeling dirty outdoor gloves off his hands. He dropped something and quickly retrieved it, stuffing the dirty plastic object in his pocket. A pill bottle? I couldn't tell; he had moved too fast.

"Surely you don't take care of all the grounds, too?" I asked.

A wary look crossed Lewis's face. "No, no, of course not. I just needed to work off some stress. There are a couple of flower beds that were Hazel's favorites. I wanted to be sure they were mulched. Who knows what's going to happen to the place now?"

"So why do the police think you would have done it?"

"Who knows? Because I was here. Because it's easier to pin it on me than to do the work to find out who really killed her. Because she left me a crummy little legacy that probably won't even exist when all her debts are paid." He was angry now.

"Who do you think killed her?"

"You were here. It's obvious, isn't it? The kid. He wanted money, and the only way to get it was to sell off the assets of the estate. And that couldn't happen as long as Hazel was alive."

"How do you know?"

"Everybody knows. It was all in Jake's will. The whole family knows it. There's barely been enough money to scrape by for years, and as long as Hazel was alive, there was nothing anybody could do — except maybe release one more greatest-hits CD."

"But how did he do it? Did he go inside after we left?"

"He must have. He left, sped off mad as a hornet because I wouldn't let him in to harass Hazel. But then I went to run some errands. He knows his way around here. He wouldn't have had any trouble getting in."

"What about the housekeeper?"

"How long did you ring the bell when you came?"

"I don't know, several times. It did seem that we waited a long time. I remember we talked about it."

"She can't hear, at least not well. Jay could have been in and out without her even knowing. And besides, that was her evening off. She was gone when I got back."

"Was that normal, for you all to leave Hazel here alone?"

"Sure. She wasn't an invalid or senile."

"And you didn't go in to check on Hazel immediately when you got back?" I suddenly saw that still, gray face propped awkwardly against pillows. I was feeling worse and worse about this. Had she already been dead when I opened that door?

"No, not right away. I was putting things away, watching the six o'clock news, having a drink. The housekeeper had left supper ready, so I put it on the tray to take in to Hazel."

"Did she always eat in her room?"

"No, but that day she had stayed in bed all day. She wasn't really sick. Sometimes she would say she had a headache and stay in bed, popping pills and drinking. It's a wonder she hadn't died before from some interaction. Nobody could make her stop.

148

When she stayed in her room all day like that, she generally had supper there, too, if she ate at all."

"Did you tell the police all this?"

"Of course, but they know I was here in the house. I don't have a lot of money or friends with power. They want this cleared up. I'm an easy target."

"What will you do now?"

"I don't know. For now, I guess things will just go on as they are. At least until the estate's settled. Until Jacqueline decides about selling the house, somebody has to take care of things. I'll find something."

"Did anybody see you while you were gone?

"What?"

"When you were gone, running errands. That afternoon."

Sudden anger replaced the bewilderment on his face. "What are you insinuating? I don't have to defend myself to you! You'd better leave. Now!"

I realized suddenly what a vulnerable position I was in and decided to take his advice and get out of there.

As I drove away, I passed a plain, dark sedan parked on the grass just outside the rear entrance. One man was in the car. It might have been the detective, but I couldn't be sure. Had he followed me, or was I just being paranoid?

My excursion meant that I was right in the middle of peak rush-hour congestion on the way home. I knew better than to get on 440 at that hour, so I headed across Harding Place. There was a wreck on the bridge over I-65, though, so I was stuck with nothing to do but listen to lame drive-time radio jokes and think.

Who knew about that back entrance to the Miller grounds? Everyone who lived there, of course. Jacqueline, Jay, probably anyone who had been around the house much. Delivery people. The delivery men Kenneth Elliott used, for instance. And, of course, I found it without much trouble, so how hard would it be if you were intent on robbery or murder? The problem with the robbery motive, though, was that nothing seemed to have been taken. As far as I knew, the only things taken from the Miller house that day were the paintings Doug and I had reclaimed for Kenneth's gallery.

By the time I had passed Harding Mall, I had decided that the Spider definitely needed a tune-up.

There were too many possibilities involved in Hazel's death. They couldn't be systematically eliminated. The thing to do would be to concentrate on the probabilities. It was probable that whoever killed Hazel had reasonable access to the house, knew Hazel and her habits, and had something to gain.

Who had access? George Lewis, Jacqueline, the housekeeper, Jay, regular tradespeople. I supposed I would have to include Doug's brother, Kenneth. Who would have something to gain? Jacqueline and Jay, of course. Lewis? Not much that I could see. Ditto for the housekeeper. Kenneth? All he wanted was to get the paintings back, and Doug and I had seen to that.

The next day, Friday, I was too busy to think about anybody's murder except maybe the wholesaler who had told me he had forty-seven seats to Tegucigalpa confirmed when he really only had them requested. I had quoted the price to my client in good faith, and now the seats might not be available. I checked other airlines, other wholesalers for a backup, but I couldn't find as good a price. I decided to give him another two days and crossed my fingers that the seats would come through.

About lunchtime, I tried to call Kenneth at the gallery. There was no answer, so I left a message on his voice mail: "Kenneth. This is Campbell. Did you get my messages? Call me, please." I stayed busy the rest of the day; we all did. Kenneth probably couldn't have gotten through the busy phone lines if he'd tried. By the time we closed I was tired, ready to go home and forget about travel for the weekend.

Stick and Randy played a nine o'clock set at the Bluebird that night. I got there just before they started and listened from a seat in the corner. Since I didn't know anyone else there, I didn't have to try to make conversation over the noise. I could focus on the music and only the music. This was why I like living in Nashville. Any night of the week you could go somewhere and hear live music. It's not about drinking or eating; it's not even about production and costumes. It's about the pure goodness of the music.

During their break, Stick and Randy headed my way, distracted by fans wanting autographs and musicians wanting to talk, ask questions, feel that they belonged in the same world with these two successful musicians, wanting the magic to rub off.

"You sound great," I told them when they finally made it over to my table.

Paul Gregg from Restless Heart was across the room, and the rumor was that

Restless Heart was looking for material for a new album. He nodded and raised a hand. Stick waved back and started toward him.

Randy sat. "Well, I take it as a good sign that you haven't run out of the room yet," he said. The table was tiny, and the room was crowded. Our knees touched.

"It's early yet."

He laughed. A waitress brought him a drink. "Thanks." He nodded. "You want something?" he asked me.

"No, I'm fine."

"Hey, Randy." A brunette with big hair stopped in front of the table. "Dallas Ray. We met backstage at the Ryman last month. The breast-cancer benefit."

"Oh, yeah, how you doing?"

"Great, great. You?"

"Plugging along. Good to see you."

It sounded to me like he was just being polite, trying to dismiss her, but she wasn't going anywhere. And maybe it was all in my head.

Silence. Well, silence except for the deafening noise all around us.

"Well, hey, I've got a CD I'd like to drop off for you," she said.

"Well, sure, but I don't —"

"I just thought you might need a girl singing some harmony next time you're playing a benefit like that. I love your stuff. I'd love to do it."

"Yeah, I guess. I mean, I usually just get up there on my own or with a few of the guys. Just leave me a card. I'll lose a CD."

"Sure." She pulled a card out of a skintight pocket like a magician pulling a rabbit out of a hat. "There. Call me anytime. I'll send you a CD, too."

She glanced at me as she left, the first time she'd seemed to notice I existed.

"Sorry," he said.

I nodded. I'd been around Stick enough to witness that kind of scene before. Competition in the music business is tough. Who knows what contact might be the one? And the girl had to know that people, the right people, listened to Randy's songs. So if they were listening to Randy and heard her . . . People had done far more bizarre things than interrupt a conversation to get noticed in this town.

Stick reappeared. "Time to get back to work."

Randy smiled an apology and shrugged as he stood up.

Oh, well, it was nice while it lasted.

It was after eleven and smoke was hanging low in the room when the boys finished their set. They packed up the equipment; I helped with the light and less-fragile stuff.

"Okay," Stick said. "Jay Miller's playing tonight at 328. As soon as we get this stuff packed up, we'll all go over there." Good. Randy was coming, too.

"Really? Thanks. You think he'll still be there?"

"Should be. They do a late set on weekends."

The drive from Green Hills to 328 Performance Hall took less than ten minutes on the nearly empty late-night streets. The club was about half full, and the three of us found seats near the back.

It wasn't my favorite style of music, but they weren't bad. You could hear the words, and the words made sense. Jay Miller, so unimpressive offstage, had an onstage presence that convinced me that Jake Miller really was his biological grandfather. Under the lights, his face had something of the haunted quality of early Jake Miller photographs. And even in music so different from songs like "Last Lonesome Train," there was something special about his voice that reminded me of Jake.

It was almost impossible to make conversation, so we just sat and listened. Randy and Stick occasionally raised an eyebrow or nodded over an impressive riff or run.

About midnight, as their next to last song, Alternative Music City did an arrangement of Jake Miller's "Saturday Night in Town." Oddly, the song fit their style, or maybe it's just that a really good song is bigger than any one style.

When they finished their last song and started to pack up, Stick turned to me. "Now what?"

"Now I'll just ask him a few questions — and hope he doesn't turn and run." I was counting on Jay's investment in his equipment to keep him from running. I knew what mattered to musicians.

We walked over to the stage, and I approached Jay from behind. He was bending over, unplugging cables.

"Excuse me," I said as nonthreateningly as I could.

He turned as he straightened up. He could hardly have run when he saw me without falling into expensive equipment. The alarm I saw in his eyes, though, was unmistakable.

"What do you want? And who are you?"

I heard an echo of the anger I had heard and seen in his grandmother's driveway.

"My name is Campbell Hale." I was speaking very calmly, glad to know that Stick and Randy were standing right behind me. Jay looked over my shoulder and nodded at Stick. Anybody in the music business would recognize Randy and Stick. If you were trying to make it in this town, you wouldn't want to make enemies of guys that successful and well liked. That fact, more than the mere physical presence of two men, gave me confidence and made me feel safe.

I spoke without taking a breath. "I was at your grandmother's house the afternoon she died. I wanted to talk to you about it. I liked your music, by the way. You're good."

"For what that's worth in this town." I couldn't help wondering what had made Jay Miller so bitter so young. "So what? What business is it of yours?"

"Not much, I guess, except that I was there that day, and I've been questioned by the police. I'm just trying to put it all together in my mind." I didn't mention that I'd actually seen his grandmother. "I didn't know who you were when I saw you, but I know Lewis wasn't about to let you in. I'd say that clears you. I, on the other hand, was inside the house that afternoon, and part of the time I was alone."

As I had hoped, he softened some after that, but I could feel Randy and Stick staring at me.

"Yeah, well, Lewis had no right to keep

me out. Hazel's my grandmother, *was* my grandmother, and I had every right to see her, a lot more than some paid flunky."

"Did Lewis usually control who saw your grandmother?"

"Not like he did that day. Sometimes I'd go by, and he or the maid would say she was asleep or didn't feel like seeing anybody, which usually meant she was drunk or stoned. But nobody had ever tried to keep me out of the house before."

"Why were you there that day?"

He looked at me for a long minute. "I needed Hazel's help. I'm this close to a record deal." He held up his thumb and index finger. "The head of the label is an old friend of Jake and Hazel's. I knew Hazel could talk him into the deal. But she had to talk to him then — before somebody made a different decision."

"But you were already mad when you got there."

"I called first. I don't usually, but I needed to know if she was conscious. Lewis told me I couldn't come, couldn't see her. I went anyway."

"So what happened? After I left, I mean?"

"I didn't get in. I yelled some more and stomped around, and then I left. I decided it was pointless trying to yell my way in. If

Hazel was drunk or doped up, which was what I figured, she couldn't help me right then anyway. If Lewis and I had a fight, Hazel would be upset and not in the mood to do a favor. I decided I'd come back the next morning, take her to the Pancake Pantry for breakfast. She'd see people who knew her, people from the business. Somebody there would recognize her. She'd feel like a celebrity, and she might want to prove she could still move and shake a little."

"You didn't try to go around to the back?"

He looked sideways and noticed a band member packing up. "Man, be careful with that. I get that guitar neck sprung, I'll never get it back right. Just leave it. I'll get it myself." He turned back to us. "That's one of Jake's guitars, an old Martin. It has the sweetest sound. You can't find anything like it now." He shook his head. "Hazel gave it to me."

He seemed more at ease, talkative and cooperative. I took a risk. "What about the estate? There must be a lot of money involved if some of those assets were sold. That could stake a struggling new band."

Randy put his hand on my arm. Stick stepped closer to me. I saw sudden fire in Jay Miller's eyes.

"Just what are you trying to pull, lady?

159

Hazel was my grandmother, my family! I wouldn't kill her for money. There's only one Hazel Miller. And anyway she was worth a lot more to me alive than dead. What do you want here anyway?"

"I'm sorry," I placated. "I can see that, and surely the police can, too. What do you think happened?"

"I don't know. I'd like to pin it on Lewis. He was right there; he controlled who saw Hazel and who didn't. He's a self-important little jerk. I could never stand him, and I guess he feels the same about me. But I don't know. I think he really cared for her. He really thought he was protecting her all these years."

"From whom? You?"

"Lawyers who wanted to steal her paintings, maybe?"

He had me there. "Maybe," I conceded. I guess someone had told him who Doug and I were and why we were there. "What about your mom? How did she and Hazel get along? Did she ever say anything about Rosie Layne? I heard she sang backup for your grandfather for a while?"

"You don't really think I'm going to talk to you about my mother, do you? Look, I don't know who killed Hazel, and I'm tired of people gettin' off on talking about my family. My mom's had to put up with this all her life. I'm sick of it. You people are like vultures. Get out of here."

We took his advice. I always seemed to go one question too far. As we crossed the street to the vacant lot where we had parked, I thought I saw the dark sedan again.

"Satisfied?" Stick looked disgusted.

"I guess. I think I believe him, but I'd hate to be a sick and drunk old lady who made him mad. He has some serious anger issues."

"Did I miss something? Did somebody make this your business? One woman is dead. Are you trying to double the stakes?"

"Stick! I just wanted to talk to him. And I don't really think he did it."

"Well, somebody did it, and you're out there stirring things up. That's stupid!"

"Thank you for going with me." I was contrite; I was apologetic. I was glad I had done it.

"Count me out of your schemes next time."

"Okay." I was meek. Stick was unconvinced. Randy was quiet.

We drove back to the Bluebird, where I had left my car. Randy walked me to the car. Stick was still fuming.

"Will you be okay?" Randy asked.

"Yeah, I'm fine. Thanks. Really. Thanks for going."

"Anytime. Well, actually, I think Stick's right. You don't need to put yourself in danger." Changing the subject, he said, "But I would like to go out again — without a murder suspect, I mean. Okay if I call you?"

"Yes, I'd like that."

"Okay. I'll call you, then. Be careful."

"I will."

"Nice car. How long have you had it?"

"For years, since college. It was my first car."

"I like it." He stood there smiling as I drove off.

Was he smiling at me or the car? He's a nice guy. *Just have fun being with a nice guy.* How many times had I told myself that?

Had Jake Miller had two old Martin guitars? Because I was sure I'd seen one in Jake's shrine room that could have been the twin of the one Jay had played tonight. If it was the same guitar, when could Hazel have given it to him? He would have had to have stolen it at some point after we left the house. And he never did answer my question about the back entrance.

CHAPTER NINE

There's a time in the night that won't listen to lies, A time when your heart waits for mine.

— Jake Miller,
"The Sound of My Heart Breakin' "

I slept in Saturday morning, missing my weekly HGTV fix. Watching HGTV makes some people feel guilty, guilty because even when they manage the time to cook something, it isn't from scratch. Their herbs aren't fresh because they haven't grown them from seed. If they're using cloth napkins, it doesn't count because they didn't hemstitch them personally from Irish linen and monogram them by hand.

It's different for me. It's like taking teenagers to night court to scare them away from dangerous behavior. It's like seeing the terrible damage of alcoholism and vowing never to take a drink. Thirty minutes of

HGTV every Saturday morning, and I can use paper plates to serve microwaved food without a lick of guilt.

But this Saturday, having slept too late for my fix, I got up and decided to make eggs Benedict.

Eggs Benedict is my favorite breakfast food, and I keep trying to find the perfect hollandaise recipe. Give me a double boiler and a decent balloon whisk, and I can give you a hollandaise, but I have trouble with consistency. The story of my life.

First, of course, I toast the English muffins. Good quality sliced bread, toasted, will even do in a pinch. When I saw there were no English muffins, I knew I was in a pinch. I toasted the bread and slipped it into the oven to stay warm.

I poured orange juice into a champagne glass to sip while I cooked. The sun was shining; little, colorful birds of whose names I was clueless were stuffing themselves at the feeder. My mockingbird was on duty in his dogwood. I put a couple of slices of Canadian bacon on top of the toast in the oven to take the chill off. I could hear the distant hum of a motorboat on the river, its hull slapping the water. I put egg yolks, melted butter, and lemon juice in the top of the double boiler. I began to whisk. No problem. I can do this, I told myself. I put a little more lemon juice. I whisked.

The biggest problem I have is poaching eggs. Martha Stewart says you should have fresh country eggs, but I'm stuck with whatever's at the grocery store. Sometimes my poached eggs break, or the whites mush out in the water, or they're too hard. I've tried poaching rings, poaching spoons, poaching pans. I've tried gently swirling the eggs as I delicately slide them into the water. Sometimes it works; sometimes it doesn't. Kind of like life.

One time, though, I saw an episode where Martha poached eggs. She used a piece of bread, an end slice, to blot the water. My mother would have been horrified at the idea of such waste. Then Martha trimmed the edges of the egg whites. She trimmed the edges! I could have even edges if I trimmed them!

Today everything worked. A good omen. I slid the unbroken eggs on top of the Canadian bacon, and all was well with the world. I spooned the hollandaise on top, a dash of paprika for color, and I took my breakfast and the paper out on the patio. This was what Saturday morning was supposed to be.

I was finishing the sports section of *The*

Tennessean when the phone rang.

It was Mark. "Just thought I'd warn you. There's going to be a feature in Metro/State tomorrow on the Miller thing." The Metro/ State was the news section of *The Tennessean.* "It'll talk about the grandson's being there that afternoon, attributed to unnamed sources. I don't think your name will be mentioned, but I'm not sure about Doug's. Thought you'd want to know. There'll be a lot of background stuff — Jake's career, his and Hazel's marriage. There's some stuff about their art collection, Doug's brother's gallery. You know, 'surprisingly cosmopolitan collection for a country-music singer,' that kind of thing."

"Great." My voice was heavy with sarcasm. "Doug will love that. Will it be in the early editions?"

"Yeah. You can get a copy at Walgreens about midnight."

"Thanks. I think I'll do that. Thanks for the heads-up, Mark."

"Anytime, kiddo."

A cloud of little cedar waxwings descended on the dogwood. The mockingbird went berserk, screeching first at one, then another. He could scare off one or two at a time, but there were too many for him, and he was overpowered. He whooshed by my

166

chair, still screeching. Demanding my help, maybe?

"Sorry," I shrugged. "You're on your own." I went inside.

MaryNell came by later that day.

"You need a dog," she announced.

"No, I don't. Why?"

"You wouldn't live alone if you had a dog; you'd have a companion. Besides, men like dogs. They find women with dogs very attractive."

I opened my mouth to answer that, but too many bad and cynical jokes were competing. I shut it. Then a light dawned. "Your dog's having puppies?"

She looked at me. "Well, yes, but that's beside the point."

"I don't want a dog."

"You need a watchdog."

"I have an alarm system, and I've practiced dialing nine-one-one very fast."

"Wait until you see how cute they are. I won't even say I told you so when you change your mind."

I stood firm. I was resolute. She gave up, but I knew it was only temporary. The puppies weren't even born yet. We talked over Mark's heads-up about the article. MaryNell thought I ought to warn Doug, and I decided she was right. I thought it would be better to do it in person, and I stopped at The Food Company just before it closed to pick up a loaf of bread as a peace offering.

After I rang his bell, I held up the bread so he could see it through the peephole. The security guard had called him from the lobby, and he hadn't told the guy to throw me out. But I could feel him hesitating, wondering if opening the door was going to be a mistake. The trouble was, I knew that when I told him the news, he'd be sure of it. I did not enjoy being an albatross to this man.

The dead bolt turned slowly. He opened the door but left the chain on.

"Hello," I said.

"Yeah?" This was uncharacteristic for Doug, almost rude.

"If you leave the chain on, the bread won't go through the door." I tried to appeal to his logical side.

"I know. I'm thinking."

"I could set it down out here and go away."

"That wouldn't prove anything. The bread could be booby-trapped."

"It's bread."

"It looks like bread. It could be a bomb."

Doug closed the door, unhooked the chain, and opened the door. "Is it a bomb or a bribe?"

"I prefer to think of it as a peace offering. Seven-grain. Your favorite."

"Which act of aggression is this for? Or is it something I don't know about yet?"

"Sort of. But I don't really think I can be blamed for this."

Doug's eyes rolled. "You never can, can you?"

"That really isn't fair. I came to warn you."

"Warn me. About what?"

"*The Tennessean*'s running a feature about the murder tomorrow — in the Metro/State section. Chronology, background, bios of all the players. You may be a player. I thought you'd like to know."

"Thanks. Now I can lose sleep tonight wondering if I'm going to be implicated in a murder tomorrow."

"Well, we could get an early edition about midnight. The twenty-four-hour Walgreens has them."

"No, thanks. Oh, what the heck. I won't be able to sleep anyway. Come on. Let's go get some dinner, and we'll get a paper later."

"You're sure?"

"Yeah. Have a seat. I'll change shirts and

be right back."

"Okay."

A football game — Vanderbilt and Ole Miss at Oxford — was on the TV. Ole Miss was up by two touchdowns and had possession of the ball. The band played "Dixie," but only in a medley with "The Battle Hymn of the Republic."

Less than ten minutes later, just as Ole Miss scored, Doug came out in pressed khakis and a starched oxford cloth shirt. Pink. A lot of men don't wear pink, but it can be a very becoming color. Doug looked really good in pink oxford. I wished he didn't, wished I didn't find him quite so appealing, but there it was. He shrugged into a navy blazer, asked if I was ready, and opened the door. I felt underdressed, but I nearly always felt a little underdressed around Doug.

"I called Kenneth to let him know," he said.

"What'd he say?"

Doug shrugged. "He didn't seem too concerned. He said somebody had called the gallery this week. Of course, the newspaper isn't going to place him at the scene of a murder. I told him I'd call him later and tell him what's in the story."

We looked at the online edition, but we

both wanted to see the actual paper. Online and print edition stories aren't always identical, and we wanted to see what would be going out in print.

We had time to kill (maybe *time to spare* would be a better choice of words) before the early edition of the Sunday paper would be out, so we went downtown to the Capitol Grille. One thing about Doug, he does choose great restaurants.

The Capitol Grille is downstairs in the Hermitage Hotel, one of Nashville's oldest hotels. It's beautiful, ornate, and elegant, but also a place that makes you want to sit back and stay a while. I had something wonderful with a white-truffle sauce. Maybe anything's wonderful with a white-truffle sauce. A pianist played quietly, and by unspoken mutual consent we ignored the murder. We talked about music, movies, a little politics, just small talk, really. I felt myself relaxing and realized this was the best time I'd had with Doug in a while. He seemed to be enjoying himself, too.

Finally, after one last coffee, we left the Hermitage, drove out Broadway, and turned toward Green Hills on Twenty-first.

"Yeah, we get 'em," said the surprisingly courteous clerk with seven earrings in one ear and unnaturally black hair above his

171

blond eyebrows, "but you're a little early." He looked at his watch. "Maybe half an hour."

We browsed while we waited. Doug and I are both readers, and we talked about books we'd read recently and wanted to read. I recommended a classic, James Carville's *We're Right, They're Wrong*. Doug thought I should read Newt Gingrich's new book.

It was the kind of warm, laughing, comfortable evening that, early in our friendship, made me think this relationship had possibilities. A time when I'd find myself smiling for no particular reason. That evening made me a little sad for what might have been but wasn't quite for reasons I hadn't completely figured out yet, for what I was beginning to admit might never be.

Then *The Tennessean* arrived, and Doug and I swarmed before the delivery man could cut the plastic binding on the top bundle of papers.

Doug's name was there: "Attorney Douglas Elliott, representing The Mockingbird Gallery, owned by Elliott's brother, Kenneth Elliott, was retrieving paintings at Mrs. Miller's request. The paintings had been leased to Mrs. Miller, according to a spokesperson for the gallery." Interesting way to put that. Still, not too bad. Nothing untrue or damaging there.

"The coroner was unable to pinpoint the exact time of death. It is unclear if Elliott was in the house before or after Mrs. Miller's death."

Doug looked grim.

Mark was as good as his word. My name didn't appear. I had a third cousin who was, when I was growing up, involved in somewhat questionable business and political activities too often for the family's comfort. He used to say that there's no such thing as bad publicity as long as they spell your name right, but I'm not sure. I was glad I was too unimportant to be worth mentioning.

We each bought a copy of the paper. Once we got back to his place I thanked a scowling Doug for dinner and headed home. It was an eerie feeling, driving those normally busy highways at that hour. There was fog, making halos around the streetlights high over 440 and the lights from the buildings downtown. The city looked darkly ominous with the Batman building and the R2-D2 building, as the two large buildings are nicknamed, standing guard over the Nashville skyline. One looks for all the world like Batman's cowl. The other looks like a giant R2-D2 robot from *Star Wars.* I kept checking the Spider's mirrors to see if anyone was following me. It's not that I haven't been out in the city that late and even later. I think it was a feeling deep in my gut that I was in the middle of something dangerous, and I was beginning to be afraid it might turn in my direction. And what about Doug? Seeing his name in print had a totally different effect than hearing it from Mark. Had the reporters made the murderer's job easier by exposing Doug as a possible police source?

When I got out to the Opryland Hotel area, lights were still blazing. Neon from the Music Valley theaters told me that I could still hear live music if I wanted to. I passed.

I pulled into my driveway under the dark canopy of trees and got out of the car. It was quiet. Too quiet. Too still. Just the hush of distant river noises and muffled traffic back by the stores and theaters.

Had I left the dead bolt locked? Yes. I thought so. I thought I remembered fumbling with the key. Burglar alarm on? Yes. I was sure. The light over my front door was on, just about twenty feet from the car. I was still standing just inside the open car door, hesitating, trying to decide if I was being silly or if I should jump back in the car and race out of there. I could go to MaryNell's. I hesitated, then leaned into the car to get my cell phone.

Something hit the car door hard, shoving it against the back of my knees and throwing me headfirst into the seat. I heard running, someone crashing through shrubbery and plants as I scrambled to get out of the car and back onto my feet. By the time I could stand, there was no one in sight. I heard a car start not far away.

I jumped in and started my own car, locking the doors as I backed and turned in a whirl of dust. I was braver in my car.

I stopped before pulling out on the road, listening to see if I could tell which direction the car fled. Left, I thought. To the right was the old water-taxi terminal and, making the forced left turn, Music Valley Drive, the most direct way out of the area. He — if it was a he — might not know that, though. To my left, the road had, decades ago, ended at a ferry that no longer existed across the Cumberland River to East Nashville (not to be confused with eastern Nashville). Now, however, the Briley Parkway bridge had replaced the ferry, and the road circled under Briley Parkway on this side of the river to connect with Pennington Bend Road and come back out on McGavock on the other side of the Opryland Hotel/ Convention Center/Music Valley Dr/ McGavock Pike exit.

Sound confusing? I was counting on that. Few Nashvillians even know the road exists, much less how it connects. I was counting on the person being afraid of getting caught at a dead end. I cut my lights but kept the engine running and waited. Suddenly the car roared by, and I peeled out after it. I was mad now. He made the sharp turn onto Music Valley, but I gained a little on him.

I tried to get close enough to read the license plate or at least make out the symbol on the back of the car. I switched on my headlights. All I could tell for sure was that it was a Tennessee plate, a plain one, six digits, no mountains, no iris, no fish, no college logo. I thought it said Davidson, Nashville's county, but that was just a guess from the length of the county name on the plate; I couldn't actually read it. The late shows must have been ending at the Music Valley theaters and clubs because cars were pouring out onto Music Valley. I lost him in the traffic. I thought I saw him turning onto Briley Parkway, but I never caught up with the car that I thought was the one. I pulled off at the Elm Hill Pike exit, turned around, and went home.

Driving back home, I suddenly realized I was sweating. Was I crazy? What had I been thinking? What would I have done if I had caught him? That's when the shakes started.

CHAPTER TEN

This time I swung the car around a couple of times, illuminating as much as possible of the front and side of the yard with the headlights. When I switched off the car I heard the normal night sounds, crickets, night birds, one of my mockingbirds singing late, all those wonderful, normal creatures that soundtrack the night.

I got out of the car and moved quickly to the door, my keys out and ready to unlock the door fast or to use as a makeshift weapon. I was halfway to the door when a dark shape emerged from the shadows, and I saw a glint of light off metal. A gun!

I screamed just before I recognized Mr. Morgan from next door.

"Sorry. I didn't mean to scare you. Are you okay?'

Mr. Morgan was patting me on the back with his gun-free hand. The other held a large, old handgun.

"Mr. Morgan! What are you doing?"

"We heard noises, saw lights and cars racing up and down the street. Mildred thought she'd seen you pull in, but she called you and didn't get an answer. I thought I'd better check things out."

I told him what had happened, at least as much as I knew, and assured him that I was okay. "I didn't even know you had a gun!"

"Mildred doesn't like for me to have it in the house. She's always afraid one of the grandchildren will get it. I got it back during the war."

The war? 1812? Northern Aggression? No, for Mr. Morgan's generation, "the war" would always be World War II.

"You ever use it?"

"Nope. Never had to yet. Better to have it and not need it than to need it and not have it."

I couldn't decide if I felt better or worse knowing Mr. Morgan was right next door with a gun that hadn't been fired in over half a century. I got inside without further excitement and locked the door behind me. I double-checked the lock, just to be sure, and started to look around.

At first I didn't see anything out of order. The lights worked. The phone was ringing.

"Campbell?" It was Mrs. Morgan. "Are

you okay?"

"Yes, ma'am, I'm fine."

"We heard noises over toward your house. Howard got his gun out and came over, but by the time he got it out of the closet and found his bullets, everything was quiet. Your car wasn't there. Is everything okay?"

"Yes, ma'am. I think I had a prowler, but he's gone. I tried to follow him, but I lost him."

"Campbell, honey! You shouldn't have followed him. Have you called the police?"

"No. Not yet. I just got in. Is Mr. Morgan back?"

"He's just walking in the door."

"Great. I'm really okay. I'll call you in the morning. Thanks."

I took the phone to my bedroom and dialed Doug's number.

"Hello?"

"Doug. Hi. This is Campbell."

"Is something wrong?"

"Somebody was at my house when I got home. Outside, I mean. I'm inside now, but I haven't looked around yet."

"Are you okay?"

"Yeah. I feel silly. I just want to make sure everything's okay. I don't think anybody's been inside."

"What happened?"

"I got out of my car, and it didn't feel right. Everything was too quiet." I told Doug what had happened. "The Morgans next door heard something. Whoever it was took off through the shrubs and, I think, got away in a big dark car. Looked expensive, but I could never get close enough to be sure of the make."

"Did you see him?"

"I didn't see the person, but I saw the car. I tried to follow, but I lost him. Her. Whatever."

"Are you sure you're all right? Have you looked around? Where are you?"

"I think I may have some ugly bruises on my legs, but otherwise I'm fine. I'm in my bedroom. Everything looks okay." The clothes and the stack of books beside the bed spilling over onto the floor were normal. I had left them that way. "I'm going into the kitchen now."

"Was your burglar alarm set?"

"Yes. And I've rearmed it."

"No windows broken?"

"No. Doug!"

"What?"

"There's writing on my windows. The big window in the den over the patio. It's red."

"What does it say?"

"It's hard to read. It's smeared some. I

think it says 'Mind your own business. . . . You could die too.' "

"Is it written on the outside or inside of the window?"

"Outside." I touched the window to be sure. "It's red, bright red."

"Blood red?"

"Don't say that! With big drips. What should I do?"

"Call the police. Then start minding your own business. I'm coming over."

"No, no. You're all the way across town. Just talk to me."

"You need to call the police."

"Okay. I'll call the police. Then I'll call you back. If I don't call in ten minutes, you call me. If I don't answer, call nine-one-one."

"You're sure you don't want me to come over?"

"No, I'm okay. I just want to know somebody will know something's wrong if, well, if something happens. I'll be fine. Okay." I was trying to calm myself. "I'm going to call the police now. I'll call right back. Thanks."

My fingers were shaking.

"I'd like to speak to Detective Davis. Somebody's vandalized my house."

"Ma'am, what's your name?"

"Campbell Hale. Can I talk to Detective Davis?"

"Your address, ma'am?"

I gave the address. "Can I speak to Detective Davis?"

"Ma'am, can I have your phone number, please?"

I was beginning to get the idea. I gave the passively aggressive dispatcher all the information she asked for. She said she'd leave a message for Detective Davis and send a patrol car to my house. I thanked her.

Then I called Doug back.

"I'm sure I have Detective Davis's home number at my office," Doug said. "It was on his card. He probably gave it to you, too. You didn't throw it away, did you?"

"No, I don't think so." I walked over to my desk as I talked and started looking through papers, bills, receipts. I emptied out my purse. I don't throw things away generally until I'm about to drown in mostly useless paper; then I get ruthless. "I found it. Okay. I'm going to call him. Thanks for thinking of that."

"Good. Call him, then call me back."

I dialed the detective's home number. There was a sleepy, feminine "Hello?" followed by an alert, undeniably masculine "Davis."

"Detective Davis, this is Campbell Hale. You talked to me about Hazel Miller's death." I wasn't breathing, just talking very fast. "Somebody was at my house tonight." I told him about the message on the window.

"Did you report this?"

"Yes. They said they'd send somebody out."

"When they get there, tell them I'm on the way. Tell them I said to wait until I get there and not to touch anything. That goes for you, too."

"Okay." I must have sounded uncertain.

"I mean it. I don't want anybody tramping around."

"Yes, sir." I had half expected him to dismiss me, tell me he'd talk to me in the morning, especially after the woman answered. But he hadn't. He was getting out of bed to come immediately. That ought to be comforting, but somehow it made it worse to know that he was worried, too.

He must have contacted the patrol car before they got to my house. When they pulled in the drive moments later, I met them on the porch. They introduced themselves. Officers McMurtry and Simmons asked my name, assured me Detective Davis would be there shortly, and started filling out forms on a metal clipboard. My name, my address, my phone number, was I the one who called, what time did I call, could I describe the person or the car, where did I work, that address, that phone.

Officer McMurtry got a roll of yellow crime-scene tape out of the patrol car and held it, twirling it in her hands. I was still answering questions when Detective Davis pulled up in the dark sedan I realized I had seen much too often lately. Another patrol car was behind him.

"Let's get the searchlights on." He was in command instantly. "Light up as much of this front as you can. Okay, Ms. Hale, tell me what happened."

"Have you been following me?"

"Not close enough, apparently."

I went through the story, explaining, pointing, demonstrating. He told the patrolmen what area he wanted taped, which basically amounted to my entire yard.

"Is that necessary?" I asked.

"It is if we're going to learn anything. If your vandal had anything to do with my murder, I want everything that might tell us anything. I don't usually get out of bed to check out vandalism." He sent one patrolman next door to talk to the Morgans and two down the road looking for the spot

185

where the car had been parked. They took more yellow plastic tape.

Detective Davis and I went inside. He looked around appraisingly, and I found myself unexpectedly wishing my dirty dishes weren't all over the counter. Detective Davis was maybe ten years older than me, just beginning to gray. He had that tired look that can fool women into thinking a man's vulnerable and open when he's really only tired. I wondered about the woman who had answered the phone, the woman he'd left at home when he got out of bed to come here.

"I'm sorry I called so late. It sounded like I woke up your wife."

"I'm not married."

"Oh."

He looked sideways at me, almost smiling. "That was my daughter."

"Oh." Single father. That was new information. I'd have to think about that.

"You said you were alone, Ms. Hale?" He had blue eyes, tired eyes right now, but nice eyes all the same. What did that mean? It wasn't just that he looked at me. It was that his eyes made a connection; they felt forgiving, accepting, that they'd give you a break when you needed one. Probably some interrogation technique. There was something, too, in the wrinkles in the corners of his eyes. This was a man who had smiled often. I like a man who smiles. Not that my track record suggested I'd had any success in judging a man by his smile. I needed to think about my intruder, not Detective Davis's comforting looks. Note to self: don't evaluate men when you're feeling this vulnerable.

"Yes. I was alone."

"Hmm." He walked over to the window, taking a closer look at the letters on the outside. Maybe an inch-wide brush. I wondered if that told us anything important. "What's under this window — soil, mulch, gravel?"

"Concrete. That's part of the patio."

He grimaced. He spoke without turning to look at me. "He, she, whatever, wrote backward so you could read it from the inside and did a pretty good job of it. You ever try to write backward? I wouldn't think it would be easy." He turned back to me. "Did you have any sense of knowing this person? Any sounds, any smells? You know, like the way you'll recognize somebody by the way he moves sometimes?"

I thought. "There's nothing I can tell you, nothing I can put my finger on, but yes, I thought it was a man."

"What about the car?"

"It was dark, kind of big, looked expensive, I think. Loud?"

"Dark, big, maybe expensive. That narrows it down."

I didn't appreciate the sarcasm. "I'm sorry." I was on the verge of becoming indignant or, worse, crying. It was late, and I was tired and losing my adrenaline rush. "I did try to follow it."

"Yes, of course you did." His eyes flashed for a second, pale, clear blue. Then they were hooded again, the intensity hidden with a studied nonchalance. "That's exactly the kind of stupid stunt that leads to people scrawling threatening messages on your windows."

"What was I supposed to do, collapse in tears while the guy got away? I had to do something. And why have you been following me? I've been seeing your car everywhere I go. I just didn't know it was yours."

"I do seem to have been following you, but not on purpose. I just always seem to be one step behind you."

"Oh." I let myself be mollified. I didn't want to make an enemy of this man. I didn't need any more enemies. This house had always seemed safe to me, a haven from the city madness. Now it didn't seem so safe.

Whoever was here hadn't been inside, but I knew he could have gotten in if he'd wanted to badly enough. Someone had been here, had stood at my window, and he wanted me to be afraid. He had succeeded.

"You know, you've been spending a lot of time messing around a murder scene," Detective Davis said. "That does attract the attention of investigating officers, not to mention the murderer. What were you doing coming out of the back exit of Hazel Miller's house?"

"I was just curious, wandering around. I saw George Lewis and talked to him a few minutes."

"And at 328? What's your connection with Jay Miller?"

"I was out with friends. I like live music. Of course, I'm curious about this whole thing. Who wouldn't be? I feel part of it."

"Somebody unpleasant seems to think you're part of it, too." He nodded toward the writing, red paint dripping like blood from the scrawled letters. "Unless there's something else you've been meddling in. You're lucky I'm the kind of guy who keeps an open mind, who doesn't jump to conclusions. A more suspicious type would wonder about your interest in Jay Miller, wonder where and when you might have met him before, wonder what you have to talk to him about, especially if you knew your way around his grandmother's house."

"I didn't know my way around! I just, just wandered." I took a deep breath. Don't get defensive, I reminded myself. "But you're not suspicious?"

"Nope. Just — curious." He went over to the blinking answering machine and raised an eyebrow at me. "May I?"

"Sure." What did I have to hide?

"I've done some checking, of course. Haven't found that you have any prior connection to any of the principals in this. Yet. Except Doug Elliott, of course." He punched the Play button.

I was coming into my anger as the tape rewound and stopped. A voice filled the room, distorted and even more alarming because the speaker had been yelling into the phone. "I've seen the paper. I told you this was none of your business. Now I'm warning you. Leave my family alone! All of us!"

It was Jay Miller. His anger hung in the air and filled my house. Did it make sense for me to be the target of his anger? I hadn't killed his grandmother. I realized he must have known about the article from a reporter who had contacted him or his mother for statements. How was it my fault? Was the writing on the window Jay's?

Detective Davis and I looked at each other. There was shock on my face. Detective Davis's look said, *See? I told you so.*

"Look, Ms. Hale, somebody went to a lot of trouble tonight to tell you they're not happy with your curiosity. Take their advice; drop it. Your tax dollars underpay me to take that risk for you. You wouldn't want the city to decide I'm unnecessary, would you? A single father, out of a job?"

"Never thought of it that way." I was trying to be light, but my voice was shaking.

"There's always another perspective. Now, let's talk about your perspective. Something you've done, somebody you've talked to, some question you've asked has upset somebody, certainly Jay Miller, although it seems unlikely that he'd announce himself like that if he'd done this." He waved an arm toward the window. "No reason to sneak around if he's going to threaten you openly. Whoever did this didn't want to be identified." He sat down with the attitude of a man making himself comfortable for a long stay and pulled out a notebook and pen. "Tell me what you've been up to lately."

I tried to remember everyone I had talked to since the murder, tried to tell him everything I could remember talking about. Uniformed officers came in a few times, conferred with him briefly, and quietly went out again.

"If Jay Miller believes you're responsible for something in the *Tennessean* story, somebody else could, too," Davis suggested.

I was almost finished when Doug walked in, looking professional and, even in khakis and a knit polo shirt, managing to suggest a three-piece suit.

"Hello. I'm Doug Elliott. I represent Ms. Hale."

"Mr. Elliott." Detective Davis shook Doug's hand and looked sideways at me. "Sam Davis. How convenient. Did I remember to read Ms. Hale her rights?"

"Is Ms. Hale a suspect?"

"I didn't think so. Of course, everyone's a suspect until the case is closed. You should know that, Counselor. But I'm glad you're here. I'd like to ask you a few questions, too. This is cozier."

I stood up. I had to get out of there. "Well, if we're all going to get cozy, I'm going to make coffee." As I left the room, I noticed that Doug was not amused.

When I brought the tray in, Doug was wearing his mulish look. Maybe *passive aggressive* is a more precise term than *mulish,* but mulish was how he looked.

Doug took his coffee with cream and three sugars, an extravagant indulgence I'd always thought didn't fit his otherwise disciplined personality. Detective Davis, of course, drank his coffee black and hot without waiting for it to cool. He looked just as intractable but more patient than Doug.

Doug, who had been trying to avoid the whole Hazel Miller situation, had less to tell than I did. And he, not having had threats scrawled on his windows, was not frightened into cooperation as I had been.

When Detective Davis went out to talk to the uniformed officer, Doug started reminding me he'd told me so. I didn't tell him about the voice mail from Jay Miller. I'd have been far more annoyed if he hadn't raced across town in the middle of the night and if he weren't, even as he fumed, checking the locks on all my windows and doors.

"You realize," I interjected, trying for humor, "that now your fingerprints are on every lock in my house. Think what trouble that could get you into the next time I have police out here dusting the place."

Doug stopped, looked at me, and said, "What makes you think I haven't thought of that? Now, when I murder you out of sheer frustration, I'll have a police homicide detective as witness that there's an innocent reason why my fingerprints are everywhere."

I don't know what it was: too much caffeine late at night, delayed reaction, a sudden realization that this situation wasn't a joke? I burst into tears, wet, noisy, unquenchable tears, then hiccups, too, just as Detective Davis returned. Doug looked stricken and far guiltier than he deserved. I felt foolish and embarrassed, and that made me cry more.

Doug hovered, unsure if touching me would make it stop or trigger a new explosion.

"Am I interrupting something?" Detective Davis angrily asked.

I took off for the bathroom. I washed my face in cold water, but every time I looked in the mirror, I started crying again. Finally, Doug knocked tentatively at the half-open door. "Are you okay?"

I slowed to an occasional sob between hiccups, but I didn't answer.

"Detective Davis said for you to drink some water. Either that or I should slap your face. I thought I'd suggest water."

I splashed my face one more time and wiped it with a towel hanging beside the sink.

"I'm sorry," Doug apologized. "I shouldn't

have said that. About murdering you. Not after all this."

I shook my head, my face still buried in the towel. Wouldn't you know it? We're finally having an intimate moment, and I have a swollen, blotchy face, standing in my bathroom, a bra on the floor and mildew on the shower curtain I'd been meaning to bleach. It was enough to make me want to start crying all over again.

"It's not your fault. It's not you," I said. "I don't know. It just hit me, I guess."

Doug looked relieved if unconvinced. "I think the detective has a few more questions if you're okay."

"I'm okay. I'm fine."

"But you don't have to tell him anything."

I nodded.

"Do you want me to check the windows back here?" He was unusually cautious, still afraid of another emotional outburst.

"Please. Yes. Thank you."

He headed for my bedroom, while I headed to the living room. Detective Davis held a glass of ice water and looked as hesitant if not as unprepared as Doug.

I took the water and sat down. "Thank you." I drank the water and held the cool glass to my face.

"You okay?" That was the question.

"Sure. I'm sorry. I don't know why that hit me just then." I took a deep breath. "Doug said you wanted to ask me more questions."

"Just a few." He looked uncertain. "Is, uh, Mr. Elliott going to stay here tonight?"

I blinked. The rest of the night. I hadn't thought that far. I knew my friend MaryNell would come in a second if I asked and never care that it was three thirty in the morning, but I didn't want to admit I was afraid. That would make it more real.

"I don't think so. We don't . . . I mean, he doesn't . . ." Talk about nobody's business. "Look, I'm really tired. Is there anything else?"

"Yeah." He held up a plastic bag with a paint tube inside. The tube had held red paint. "This yours?"

"No."

"I'm guessing this is our medium. Acrylic artist's paint. It's a step up from our normal graffiti vandal. They tend to lean toward spray paint from Kmart. At least it's water-based. Oil-based paint is forever."

Doug came back into the room. "Everything seems secure. What's that?" He spotted the empty paint tube.

"Seems to be something Ms. Hale's guest left behind. Does it mean anything to either of you?"

I shook my head. Doug's face gave nothing away, one reason why he's such a good lawyer.

Detective Davis nodded. "We'll have some patrolmen keep an eye on the place."

"Thanks."

Detective Davis gave me another of his cards. "Keep this one handy. My beeper number's on it and my home number. Cell, too. Call me. Stay out of this. And be careful."

Doug waited until the detective closed the door, checking that it was locked. "Do you want me to stay? I could sleep on the couch."

I smiled. I knew he didn't want to do that. "No. But thanks. I'll be fine. Really. Who would try anything now? Besides, whoever was here just wanted to scare me, and he's done that."

"You're sure?" Relieved. I could tell.

"I'm sure. Thank you."

I bolted the dead bolt behind him, washed my face again, pulled on a big sweatshirt, and went to bed. I was shivering but determined to return to normal. Light was already filtering around the shades before I fell asleep.

When the phone rang at seven I jolted awake.

"You okay?" It was Detective Davis, middle-aged hero of the threatened, and why did everyone keep asking me that?

"Don't you ever sleep?" I'm not usually that rude to people who are, after all, trying to help me stay alive. It must have been the sleep deprivation.

"Not when there are citizens who need protecting. We may have a fairly decent tire print, but if you don't mind, don't spread that around."

"Okay."

"And the paint? It's an artist's paint, all right, but in addition to art-supply stores and most of the college bookstores in the city, it's available at every craft store and Walmart in town. Probably a few other places we haven't thought of checking. So I don't think it'll be too helpful. No more noises last night?"

"No. Nothing. Okay if I clean the windows?"

"I think so. I think we've found out all we're going to from the windows. Look, Ms. Hale. Be smart. Don't go poking around, asking questions. You've upset somebody out there, and I don't like what happens when he's upset."

I had set my alarm for seven thirty so I could attend church, but when I got up, I felt a too-little-sleep headache coming on. I had a grapefruit-juice-and-aspirin breakfast and went back to bed. I slept easier with the sun up.

When I finally awoke again, I started laundry and turned Trisha Yearwood up loud. Doug called at about noon to check in. Nice. Nice he was thinking about me. I boiled an egg and made some coffee. I got my camera and took a picture for myself of the writing. It wasn't likely that it would tell me anything, but I wanted to record it. Detective Davis's men had photographed it, of course, but I wanted my own record. The detective had said I could clean up, so I took Windex and cleaned it off. When I came back inside and looked out, there were still red smears.

The mockingbirds were singing. Copying first one bird's song, then another, trying out new sounds. "Where were you guys last night?" I demanded. "Huh? Why didn't you get territorial then?" They ignored me and went on with their rehearsals.

I'm normally not that obsessive, but I wanted to erase the whole experience, so I got vinegar and newspaper and went back out and scrubbed again. I scrubbed until I couldn't see any trace. If the mockingbirds thought I was crazy they never said a word.

Rain moved in, and the sky went gray. I wondered if Detective Davis was out looking for my vandal.

CHAPTER ELEVEN

On a day like today, if I was sixteen,
I'd be drivin' my Chevy just to be seen.
— Jake Miller,
"I Just Want to Be Here with You"

The next day I got to work early. It was busy, as Mondays usually are. I still wanted to check with Kenneth Elliott about that museum in St. Louis for my group trip, but I couldn't reach him and left another message. I called the museum and ordered several sets of cards with reproductions of paintings from their collections, so I could send them to the people who had reserved space for the trip.

I was still a little scared by what had transpired on Saturday night. I retold the story to Lee and Martha and Anna at work. Then Caroline from the Realtor's office upstairs came in, and I had to tell it again, then Allison, a designer from the florist next door. With each telling, Saturday night's events seemed less frightening, less out of control. I was beginning to laugh about it: Doug and Detective Davis bristling at each other like territorial dogs, me tearing off after the vandal in hot pursuit, Mr. Morgan trying to find his bullets.

"What were you going to do if you caught him?" they asked.

Yeah, well, I still didn't have an answer for that one.

Despite the calming of my fear, my curiosity remained. Driving home, I cut through Curtiswood Lane, past the governor's mansion, past the house where Sarah Cannon, the Opry's Minnie Pearl, had lived across the street from Rosie Layne's mansion. *Rosie Layne's mansion.* As the crow flies, I couldn't be that far from Hazel Miller's house. I slowed down, thinking, trying to visualize the area from above, to see where Rosie Layne's house was in relationship to Hazel Miller's back entrance.

A horn honked, and I realized I was stopped in the middle of the road, blocking traffic. A tour bus. I was holding up country-music fans intent on getting to Hank Williams's house next. I moved on. It probably didn't mean anything, Rosie's living relatively near Jake and Hazel. Nashville wasn't that big of a city.

As soon as I got home, walking fast in the early dusk to the safety of the light I'd left on at the front door, I ducked inside. I had left lights on in almost every room because I didn't want to walk into a dark house tonight. Inside, I turned on my computer in the guest room and clicked on a mapping program.

I clicked my way to a map of Davidson County, focusing in on Hazel's neighborhood. Sure enough, the streets made some odd curves, and Rosie Layne's backyard was just a couple hundred yards or so from Hazel Miller's back entrance. The connection was so obvious, but I hadn't suspected it. I printed out a hard copy of the map.

In the living room, I rooted through my old videotapes for a recording of an *Austin City Limits* with country-music legends, glad I hadn't gotten rid of them after all. Rosie Layne had been in the Opry for a long time, and I remembered her being featured in the program. I probably passed it over twice, but I finally found the tape and put it in the one VCR left in the house, fast-forwarding until Rosie appeared on the screen. She talked about the early days of the Opry, the camaraderie, the long road trips before there were luxurious tour buses.

There were black-and-white clips of her early career, including one of her singing behind Jake Miller. Seeing her young and in black and white, where faces seemed to dominate without the distracting competition of brightly colored clothes, the resemblance to Jacqueline was striking. The nose, the cheekbones, but especially the smile. Hazel surely would have known whose child she had adopted and raised. Young Jay's genes might be a throwback to his grandfather, but Jacqueline was her mother's child.

Rosie Layne. Ruth B. Laine.

I typed "Rosie Layne" in my phone's search window.

Five thousand, four hundred eighty-three results.

I clicked on a country magazine site. A feature on Rosie. "Rosie Layne was born Ruth Laine, third of six children, all with Biblical names. . . ."

Ruth Laine; the petition for child support from Jake. It was a wonder there hadn't been a lot of talk about this before. Age was Rosie's best disguise. You had to compare Rosie's old tapes and the mature Jacqueline to see the resemblance clearly. If Rosie Layne were Jacqueline's mother, had she been the girl singer waiting for Jake after that gig in Louisville? Was she with Jake when he died? Did it matter after all these decades? Did it have anything to do with Hazel's death — other than to give Rosie a possible motive to want Hazel out of the way, giving her birth daughter control of Jake Miller's estate? Maybe Jacqueline knew or suspected who her mother was, and that's why she had avoided the music-industry scene.

I cleaned my window again, scrubbing away imaginary traces of the vandal's warning. I was nervous being outside in the reaching shadows, and that made me mad. I was letting this jerk take away the peace I could usually count on at home. I scrubbed harder.

I went inside, made some hot tea — Bewley's Irish breakfast from my last trip to Ireland — and, in an act of defiance, took it back outside to the patio. No cowardly rat was going to steal my river from me! Of course, now I knew that Mr. Morgan had his World War II Colt close at hand. But I did take the phone out with me. And as I sipped, I programmed the detective's number into my speed dial — just in case I ever needed to dial it quickly. I could always delete it when this ordeal was over.

On Tuesday, between checking discount

fares to Chicago and planning a Thanksgiving-week trip to Disney World for a family of eight, I thought a lot about Rosie Layne. The idea of Rosie as Jacqueline Miller's mother was new to me, but Rosie Layne had dealt with this for over forty years. How had she lived with it? She had moved — when? decades ago — almost to Hazel Miller's back door, close enough to watch the little girl she had given up grow up. Had she regretted giving up her child once she had a mansion of her own? Did she wish she had toughed it out in those early years and raised her daughter under her own roof? How had she agonized as those stories of Hazel's substance abuse had become common knowledge?

At lunchtime, I drove through Oak Hill to Hazel's house, then to Rosie's. Then I turned into the alley behind Hazel's and found my way to Rosie's from there, tracing the path from one house to the other. Lined with hedges and browning clumps of flowers, the neighborhood was quiet. As I drove, I saw neighbors in sweatpants walking in the autumn sun, docile dogs pacing them. The two houses were closer than two football fields, and no one would have thought anything of Rosie Layne walking briskly through this alley, pumping her hand weights over her head.

I pulled off and parked. I couldn't stay long. In this neighborhood, someone would call the police or their private security firm if a strange car sat parked too long. I got out and started walking. At least I could get a little exercise.

I had walked about fifty yards when I met a woman heading toward me. Fiftyish, short salt-and-pepper hair. As she approached, I slowed.

"Excuse me."

She moved farther away from me and slowed, looking at me warily.

"Excuse me," I repeated. "I'm Campbell Hale." I thought giving my name might ease her apprehension, and what did I have to lose? Whoever was after me knew who I was anyway. "I just want to ask you a few questions." I reached into my purse and flashed my IATA card; it was a travel-agent ID card, had my photo, and looked vaguely official. "What can you remember about the afternoon Hazel Miller died?"

She crossed the road and walked faster, not making eye contact with me.

I walked on. A half block later I crossed the road to speak to a woman walking — or being walked by — a miniature pinscher. It snarled protectively at me.

"Excuse me." I flashed my meaningless ID again. "I'd like to ask you a few questions about Rosie Layne."

She glared at me and allowed the pinscher, who didn't know he was miniature, more leash.

I backed off and walked to my car, feeling stupid. Nashville has the reputation for being one of the friendliest cities in the nation, or at least we hear that on local news every now and then. I certainly couldn't prove it by these people. Of course, in a neighborhood as privileged as this one, I should have expected them to be protective of their own privacy and their neighbors'.

After a drive-through Burger King lunch, I was stuck on the phone at work until after everyone else had left, so I had to face the dark parking lot alone. I hate the earlier sunset in the fall; I don't like going out from work to my car after dark. Somehow it feels more vulnerable than going shopping or out to eat after dark.

A shadowy figure leaning against my car seemed to justify all those half-dismissed fears. I shifted my keys in my hand to position them as a weapon and started calculating whether I could unlock the office door, get back inside, and relock it before he could reach me. I kept meaning to take a self-defense course, but I never got around to it. I had a sudden vision of MaryNell standing by my intensive care–unit bed, saying, "I told her to get a dog and take tae kwon do." The shadow moved.

Should I scream? I felt my throat tighten. Could I scream? The offices on either side were closed. Would anyone hear me if I did?

The shadow detached itself from the car.

"You really shouldn't wander around dark parking lots alone."

Then I did scream.

"Sorry. I didn't mean to scare you," Detective Davis said. He didn't sound sorry. He sounded like he'd enjoyed it.

"Does being a policeman mean you get to terrify innocent people?"

"No, not innocent people. You, however, I have complaints about. It seems someone matching your description, driving an old red sports car, has been harassing the law-abiding, taxpaying, mayor-knowing ladies of Oak Hill."

"Oh."

"Yeah. You have dinner plans? Let's go get some supper, and you can talk me out of arresting you."

"Do I have a choice?"

"Sure, but with dinner you don't have to post bail when you're through."

"Where's your car?"

"Over there" — he gestured vaguely — "but I think I'll ride with you. I've never ridden with a crim— with an *alleged* criminal in a vintage red Spider. How about Carrabba's? I was going to have a sack of Krystal, myself, but in this car, I don't think so."

He wanted to know about the Spider. He asked about the torque and power-to-weight ratio. I pulled the original owner's manual from under the glove compartment, its olive cardboard cover slightly frayed at the edges. He pored over graphs of speed and rpms at each of the five forward gears and asked how fast I'd had it up to. I'd had it to 105 once on an oval track with nobody else around except a friend who worked there. The detective — "you can call me Sam if I'm not going to have to arrest you tonight" — was impressed that my dad would buy a red Spider for a girl in college. "He must have style, your dad, and he must love cars."

"I guess." I don't know that I had ever thought about it that way. Dad and Mom always had solid, reliable, large American sedans, usually white, very safe, very comfortable. Very dull. I had always thought that when my dad drove my car and fiddled with it and talked to the mechanic it was because he loved me and wanted me to be safe. He does, of course, but maybe Sam was right. Maybe he loved cars; maybe he loved this car.

Over bruschetta, Sam told me that an officer had seen a pickup driving slowly past my house. The officer was suspicious and ran the tags. It belonged to Jay Miller. Driving slowly in Nashville, however, while unusual, was not officially a crime, he said. "Well, actually, it is now, but only in the fast lane of divided highways." I told him about Doug's conversation with Franklin Polk in the courthouse stairway. He raised an eyebrow, took out his notebook, and made a few notes, then shrugged.

He looked at me long enough that I felt uncomfortable. More interrogation technique, I thought. I wanted to lower my eyes to break the contact, but I was determined not to let this man intimidate me.

"Campbell," he said finally. "Family name?"

"Yeah, grandmother's maiden name. Her parents emigrated from Inverness just before she was born."

He nodded, giving nothing away. Then he smiled. "Nice name."

Before I knew what had happened, I was telling him my life history, starting with the story of that grandmother as an accidental

211

civil-rights activist.

As a working mother in the sixties, she had had to be efficient, fitting errands into small pockets of time. She had gone to Harveys department store on her lunch hour one day, trying to pick up something, eat lunch, and get back to work in an hour. She stopped at the Harveys lunch counter to get a sandwich before dashing back to work. She waited for the waitress to notice her, but the girl stayed at the other end of the counter.

"My grandmother had no time to waste, so she kept trying to get the waitress's attention. Finally, she's running out of time and she says to the young woman on the stool next to her, 'I don't know what's wrong. I'm sure she sees me, but she won't come over. I've got to get back to work.'

" 'I think it's because you're sitting next to me,' the woman said, quiet, almost embarrassed.

"My grandmother was exasperated. She was late; she was hungry. 'Why?'

"The woman was almost apologetic. 'I'm colored.' " I laughed. "When my grandmother tells the story, she insists she hadn't noticed that before, and I always believed her. She used to say she had a one-track mind. Now we'd call her focused."

212

Sam was watching me, smiling a little, listening.

"She sat a while longer, then apologized to the woman beside her. She told her, 'I'm sorry. I wish I could sit with you all day, but I've got to get back to work. But I promise you I'll never shop here again.' She went back to work and wrote a letter to the owner about the experience, telling him exactly why she would never patronize his store again."

"Did she ever shop there again?" Sam asked.

"Not as far as I know."

She was just an ordinary working mother, helping her husband provide a home and education for her children. Her trade wasn't enough to make a difference in Harveys's bottom line.

"And that store closed years ago," he said and laughed.

Except for the sermon about minding my own business, not obstructing justice, and letting the police do their jobs, not to mention acting like I have a grain of sense and not putting myself in stupidly dangerous positions, dinner was sort of fun.

He told me about his daughter, a high-school sophomore, who lived with him. He'd been divorced for seven years, liked movies and fishing, but rarely had enough time to do either.

It seemed that Metro's finest hadn't figured out that Jacqueline Miller was Rosie Layne's biological daughter. "We still don't know that's true," Sam insisted after I explained my theory. I quietly gloated; he looked annoyed. The detective and his staff had talked to everyone in the neighborhood, including those who lived or walked near the alley. The police had asked them to call if they remembered anything else or if anything unusual or suspicious happened.

Apparently they considered a strange woman with questionable identification asking questions on the street to be unusual *and* suspicious. They had called.

The police had already talked to Jacqueline, of course, but they would check her account of where she had been and with whom on the day Hazel had died. And they would talk to Rosie Layne and make another round of the neighbors with some new and more specific questions.

I drove Sam back to my office, where his car was parked. He put his hand on my shoulder, started to say something, then stopped. I waited.

He patted my shoulder. Like my dad. "Be careful. Don't do anything stupid. Somebody — besides me — doesn't like you poking around in this." He tapped my car affectionately as he climbed out and closed the door. He got into his own car and watched as I drove off.

Something was nagging at me. Something about seeing him in his car reminded me of my vandal speeding away. It wasn't that I thought Detective Davis was the vandal, and the car I had glimpsed that night certainly wasn't his. He drove a plain, conservative, nondescript, government-issue sedan. It looked anonymous, almost invisible. No, it wasn't that, but my mind was insisting that I knew something, something important.

I tried to remember on the way home, driving across 440, slowing for the never-ending construction, but the more I tried to pin down the memory, the further it seemed to slip from my grasp.

My fumbling hadn't produced anything. Zilch. I hadn't eliminated anyone. And Sam was right. I was obviously annoying someone. Someone didn't want me asking questions. I wished I could figure out who was annoyed with me — besides the annoying detective, of course, and Franklin Polk; and Jay Miller, who insisted I was victimizing him; and Doug, as usual; and Stick.

At home, everything looked secure. I had

215

left lights on inside, outside. I gathered up my things — tote bag with work papers, purse, newspaper, keys — before I opened the car door. As I hurried to the house, I heard a car driving by slowly. I turned as I was unlocking the front door, surprised at how afraid I was. It was Detective Davis. He had followed me home. He lifted a hand to wave, and I went inside.

I couldn't decide whether to be annoyed with him for frightening me or grateful that he'd followed me home. I couldn't quite get to grateful, but I knew I felt a little more secure knowing he was paying attention. I couldn't help wondering if he gave that sort of protection to everyone.

CHAPTER TWELVE

On a day like today, if I was just seven,
I'd lie on my back, watch the clouds in the
heavens.

— Jake Miller,
"I Just Want to Be Here with You"

The message light on my answering machine was blinking. I looked for a pen and pad and sat down to listen. I have a love-hate relationship with answering machines. Without one, I'd feel that I was missing life-changing, destiny-driven messages. But I hate that feeling when I come in from a long day or vacation to the nagging blinking of that light. There are people who've called, it says, people who want me to do something, say something. People who know me well call my cell phone. But no matter how tired I am, I can't ignore that light. It might be a client stuck somewhere. Silent. Blinking. Demanding. *You asked for this,* it says. *You asked them to leave a message. You said their calls were important to you and that you'd call back.* All this, plus I had been a little afraid of my answering machine since that angry message from Jay Miller.

I had fourteen messages, three from clients. One needed a ticket to leave for Charlotte on the early flight in the morning. That was going to mean more phone calls, but it wasn't a problem. Another was leaving on a cruise in four weeks and didn't have documents yet. She had paid for this cruise months ago and couldn't understand why they hadn't sent her tickets. The third was ticketed to leave at 6:24 the next morning and needed to change his ticket. His meeting was still on, but it had been moved from Houston to Dallas. And, by the way, had he told me to reserve him a car? He needed one, but now he needed it in Dallas, not Houston.

Two were from my mother, who is afraid she'll catch me driving if she calls my cell. One was from my friend MaryNell. I'd missed a call from her on my cell earlier. Did I want to go to a movie this afternoon after work? We could make it a matinee at Green Hills or Opry Mills and save a few bucks. Too late for that.

One was from church, letting me know

about a death in the congregation. One was from a woman in my book club letting me know that next month's book would be *Moby-Dick*. Did I need a copy? Two were from telemarketers; they'd be calling me back.

Three were hang-up calls, numbers blocked from caller ID.

One was from Rosie Layne.

"I understand you've been making certain inquiries about me," said the dignified voice, eerily like and unlike the stage voice I was so familiar with. "I am at a loss to understand why, but I would prefer that you talk to me rather than to my neighbors. I will call again later."

Guess she didn't want to leave her number.

I handled the clients, called my mom, then found my copy of *Moby-Dick* and took it to the tub with a cup of tea. I poured in lavender bath gel, and it wasn't long before I was nodding into my bubbles, Queequeg getting mixed up with Jay Miller and that wax statue of Jake becoming a huge whale tattooed in rhinestones. It was time to go to bed.

At seven the next morning the phone rang.

"Miss Hale?"

"This is she," I answered.

"Rosie Layne."

"Yes, ma'am," I stuttered.

"You may come to my house this morning. Will eleven do?"

"Yes, ma'am." Maybe I should have told her I'd have to check my day planner, see if I could fit her in, but somehow I didn't think it was really a question.

"Very well. I assume you know where I live." Her voice was heavy with sarcasm as she hung up.

At seven minutes before eleven I parked in the circular drive in front of Rosie Layne's house. As I rang the bell, I noticed the security camera focused on me. I was nervous. Should I ignore it or look it in the eye? Would looking at it make me seem too conscious of it, as if I were checking out the security, casing the joint? Would avoiding it make me seem as if I had something to hide? I waited and tried to appear poised and keep myself from fidgeting.

At 11:01, the door opened and a woman of about Rosie Layne's age appeared, matronly and neatly dressed. "Yes?"

"I believe Ms. Layne is expecting me. I'm Campbell Hale." The left eyebrow rose. The woman reminded me of a particularly intimidating librarian at my high school,

Mrs. McKeever. Unseen monitors of security cameras might intimidate me, but I had learned to face Mrs. McKeever's worst years ago, matching the woman's gaze, steady and unblinking. *Yes, I have a pass. I am supposed to be here this period.*

"Yes. You may wait in the library." The library! I knew it. She held the door as I entered, then closed it behind me. She crossed the marble hallway quickly and I followed, the sound of our shoes on the marble floor breaking the silence in the house.

She led me into a sunny room with book-lined walls, raised the eyebrow once again, and left, shutting me in. I looked around the room as I waited. Rosie's house was very different from Hazel's. There were framed album covers, posters, and gold records, but they weren't the focus of the room. The upholstery was bold, bright florals. Matching love seats flanked a fireplace and faced each other across an Aubusson rug. A leather wing chair stood beside a piecrust table by a tall, wide window. Another was across the room near the door. Small occasional tables held lamps and waited for cups of tea, books put down for a moment of conversation. Leather ottomans were nearby. Strategically placed floor lamps suggested that this room was actually intended for reading and the comfort of readers. The books were new and old, hardback and paperback; they looked read. The windows were large with sheer curtains pulled wide and valances matching the upholstery. It was a warm room, tasteful, friendly.

Rosie entered the room and matched it. Unlike her brash, hillbilly stage persona, the at-home Rosie wore crisply creased camel wool slacks with a persimmon sweater over a beige silk blouse. She definitely looked more Oak Hill than Ryman.

"Miss Hale. I'm Rosie Layne."

"Yes, ma'am." I didn't seem to be able to say much else to her.

She sat on the love seat across from me. "My neighbors tell me you're interested in my activities. May I ask why?"

Suddenly, facing her directness, I felt like nothing more than a busybody in need of a life. Her unspoken question — what business was it of mine? — hung in the air between us. Failing other options, I decided to be honest.

I told her about being at Hazel's that afternoon with Doug, about finding Hazel's body, about some of my conversations and theories, then about the "visitor" who had made me too angry to give up. Finally I told her about making the connection between her and Jackie.

The muscles in her jaw softened as she listened. She was clearly ill at ease, but not at all fidgety. On the contrary, she had an extraordinary stillness.

"Miss Hale, let me assure you, I didn't murder Hazel Miller. If I were going to kill Hazel Miller, I'd have done it decades ago. She had some hold over Jake, not enough to keep him faithful, but enough to keep him coming home."

She sighed and went to the door. "Hannah. Would you bring us some tea, please?" She crossed to the window and stared out until the woman with the eyebrow returned and served us. Neither of us spoke.

"Thank you, Hannah." Hannah left.

"Most of your theories are close. Jacqueline is my daughter. And Jay is obviously Jake Miller's grandson. Jake said he would support Jacqueline, but only if I let him and Hazel adopt and raise her.

"I was opening for Jake, and we were playing West Memphis, Arkansas. I waited in the car while Jake and the band packed up and put away the equipment. He came out and signed a few autographs, still on an applause high from the crowd. He kissed me, but he wasn't kissing *me;* he was being Jake

223

Miller. He was always like that after a show that went well — high on being himself. We started driving toward Nashville, but when we got to Memphis, Jake decided we would stop and spend the night at the Peabody. It was beautiful, unlike any place I could afford to stay in back then, better than I could even dream of except as the woman with Jake Miller. You can't imagine. Jake registered, paid in cash up front. We went upstairs. He told me he loved me, and I told him I was three and a half months pregnant. I thought he would tell me he would see his lawyer the next day to divorce Hazel so he could marry me, and we'd live happily ever after, recording hits and raising our children. I was nineteen and naive." Her smile was sad.

"Jake was . . . sympathetic; he was apologetic. It was his fault; he would be responsible. He would take care of it. He took five hundred-dollar bills out of his wallet. He said he didn't think it would take that much, but it was all he had on him. I could probably get it done here in Memphis."

She stopped and drank her tea. She looked down and took a deep breath, shuddering.

"That was a lot of money. An abortion wouldn't have cost half that, and that's what he meant. I couldn't believe it. I had been so sure he would be happy *with* me. I was devastated. He was surprised. He couldn't leave Hazel. He'd thought I understood that."

She looked into my eyes, and I understood the strength of restraint.

"No, if I were going to kill Hazel, that's when I would have done it. I couldn't stop crying. That didn't fit Jake's mood, and it didn't fit Jake's image of himself — ruining the innocent girl. He emptied his wallet, kept just enough for gas money home, and left. He told me to stay there, rest, get myself together, and take a bus home the next day. He'd be in touch. I couldn't stop crying. I cried all night.

"Then the next day, I boarded the bus to Nashville. It took nearly all day, stopping at every little town. I can still see the signs — Arlington, Brownsville, Lewis, Cedar Grove, Huntington, then crossing the river to Mc-Ewen, Dickson, Pegram. My head hurt terribly from crying and lack of sleep.

"I was sure he had thought it over and changed his mind. I'd just taken him by surprise. Every stop was that much longer before I could see Jake. When I arrived in Nashville and went to my apartment — just a room, really — my landlady had an envelope for me. It was from Jake. Ten hundred-dollar bills this time. I tried to reach him for over a week. He wouldn't take my calls, wouldn't see me.

"For the next couple of months I worked in town, singing demos and backup as much as I could. When I started to show, I left. That's what you did back then. Either you left town to have an abortion — illegally, of course, but everybody knew somebody who knew somebody who knew where to go — or you left town to have the baby. I went to my aunt's in Macon. I couldn't go home; then everyone would know. When the baby was born, I wrote him. I thought if he knew it was a baby, a little girl, a person, he'd want her. And he'd want me. I was just nineteen, and I was stupid enough to believe that's how things worked.

"He called me back — said he couldn't humiliate Hazel by publicly supporting a child, but if I'd let him and Hazel adopt her, she would never want for anything. I was broke. I had to work. I couldn't work and raise this child, this precious, perfect child, by myself. I cried for another two weeks and then agreed. I asked him just to give me two months.

"In the meantime, I nursed her and talked to her and sang to her. I tried to squeeze a lifetime of love into those two months. I had this foolish idea that one day she would hear me sing and remember and know that I was her mother. She wouldn't hate me because she would remember and know that I loved her. I know it seems ridiculous now." She shook her head.

"I didn't know Hazel was an alcoholic then. Maybe she wasn't then. I did hate her when she was raising my daughter and not loving enough to give up bottles and pills. I despised her. I don't know how much Hazel knew and when she knew — or suspected. Did she know from the beginning or only after she saw Jackie growing up and began to see Jake in her little face? When I could I bought this house to be near Jackie. I'd walk past their backyard and hear her laughing in her tree house. I'd see her swinging too high on her swing set. But I never saw Hazel out there playing with her. Did I do the right thing? Who knows? If Jake had lived . . . Just before he died, I thought . . . Well, at the time, I didn't think I had a choice. Franklin Polk did the dirty work. He was Jake's lawyer, just Jake's hired hand. I know if I have anyone but myself to blame, it's Jake, but I have always hated that man."

She took a deep breath, then drained her teacup.

"A year or so later, Jake was playing in

Louisville. I waited for him after the show. It was surreal, just like old times except he didn't know I was out there. He was surprised to see me, but he was Jake Miller and I was one of his women. Hazel was there that night, and he didn't want her to see me. He thought — or pretended to think — I wanted more money, started peeling off hundred-dollar bills. I told him I wanted to know my daughter, and I wanted her to know me. He was mad, said we had an arrangement, although he said he didn't think Hazel much liked having a kid." She looked at me. "That's the way he said it. As if Jacqueline were a puppy or a kitten or something." She shook her head again.

"He said he missed me, though, that there was nobody else like me. He said he'd figured out how we could see each other in Nashville without anybody finding out. I don't know. Maybe I thought if I made him choose, he'd choose me. Maybe I was beginning to grow up. I said I didn't want to be some woman he hid away and acknowledged only when he felt like it. I wanted to raise my child — with or without him. He begged me to give him some time, see what he could work out. He said it would ruin us both if I didn't give him time to talk to some people, time to talk to Hazel, time to think it over. It was a strange conversation, but that was Jake. He wanted me, or said he did, but I'd have to *give him time.*"

She took a deep breath.

"He left me there in Louisville. I know Hazel was there, but I don't know what happened after that. Maybe if I'd stayed with him . . . I don't know. He wasn't drunk when he left me, but he was mad, maybe even a little scared. Scandal was different in those days. I wasn't going to give up, but the next day I heard that Jake was dead. They said he was drunk and ran off the road somewhere between here and Louisville. I don't know. But how did Hazel get back to Nashville if she wasn't with him? I didn't have any way to prove anything. Adoption records were sealed back then. No DNA tests. I went to Franklin Polk, but that was no use. The way the agreement was drawn up, there was nothing I could do. I gave up hope, but I didn't kill Jake, and I didn't kill Hazel. And I don't know why Hazel wasn't in the car with Jake when they found his body."

She looked up.

"The week after Jake's funeral I was offered a contract with a major label. Does that about answer your questions?"

I didn't know what to say. I gaped for a moment or two. "Yes, ma'am, of course. I'm sorry."

She rose and walked back to the window. "*Sorry.* Yes, well, there's a lot of *that* in the world. I can't see that it helps much." After a long moment, she continued. "I think I'd like you to leave now."

"Yes, ma'am."

I drove back to the office and worked on automatic the rest of the day.

CHAPTER THIRTEEN

Your eyes were as blue as the Tennessee
  sky
When the buds were bloomin' in spring,
And I wonder sometimes, if I'd stayed till
  the fall,
What treasures I might have seen.

— Jake Miller,
"The Sound of My Heart Breakin' "

At home there were two more hang-up messages plus one from MaryNell. I had missed out when she had called to ask if I wanted to see a movie the evening before, but her daughter had a basketball game that night, so I joined her. I needed a little normalcy, a little sense of parents watching their children grow up, being there with and for them.

MaryNell and I found seats in the not-yet-crowded McGavock High gym just before the girls' game started. At halftime

McGavock led Hillsboro 47 to 41. MaryNell's daughter, Melissa, was playing well, with three fouls, eleven points, and a lot of rebounds. She was a point guard, an aggressive player, which was probably why she accumulated fouls. I watched her jog off the court to the locker room thinking that Rosie Layne was only a couple of years older than Melissa when she was making those life-defining decisions. Where was Rosie's mother then?

When Melissa confided in me, her greatest agonies in life seemed to be over whether she wanted to play college basketball and how to wear her hair when she was sweating in a game. When Melissa really wanted to tick off her mother, she'd talk about maybe getting her nose or an eyebrow pierced, although she confided to me that she never really would: she didn't like pain, and she thought it was stupid to poke holes in your face. She just liked to watch her mother's reaction. That was when I was glad I didn't have children.

I glanced up to see Detective Davis smiling at me from across the gym, right behind the McGavock bench. After the emotional wringer I had been through all day, it was just too much for him to be following me to a high-school basketball game. I decided to make that clear to him. I told MaryNell I'd be right back, and marched around the floor to where he sat, still grinning.

"What are you doing here?" I demanded. "I haven't done anything even marginally illegal today! Can I at least go to a friend's ball game without being shadowed and harassed?"

He looked surprised, then amused as he stared past me. "Ms. Hale, I'd like you to meet my daughter, Julie."

I turned to see a McGavock cheerleader. She was tall and pretty with her father's eyes. Her hair was long and sandy; she was very neat, not too much makeup. I was mortified.

I blushed and stuttered my name, extending my hand to shake hers. "I think I've talked to you on the phone. Good game. I didn't mean to intrude."

She was politely acknowledging the introduction, assuring me that I wasn't intruding as I fled, my face burning.

I bought two Cokes and returned to MaryNell.

"Who was that attractive man you were talking to?" she asked as I handed her a Coke. "He must be a parent; nobody else comes to the girls' games. I see him a lot."

"Attractive? You think? That is Detective

Sam Davis, one of Metro's finest."

"He's your detective? Not bad. I'd let him guard my body anytime."

"He's not my detective, and he's not my bodyguard." I gave her a withering look. "I've just totally humiliated myself by accusing him of following me. He's here to watch his daughter; she's a cheerleader."

MaryNell laughed. "Oh, he's a good father and not bad looking — and he's watching you. And you have a problem with him following you?"

"I don't want to talk about it."

"Ummh. He's still watching, still smiling. Which one's his daughter?"

I snuck a quick look. "Tall, kind of blond, second from the right. Julie Davis."

"Oh, yeah. I think Melissa knows her. I've seen them talking. I think she's even been to the house. I'll check them out." McGavock is a large school, over two thousand students, but I did not doubt MaryNell's ability to ferret out any information of a personal nature.

I had trouble concentrating on the rest of the game, because I was too busy avoiding eye contact with Detective Davis. Luckily, McGavock stayed ahead, and Melissa continued to play well. Winning may not be everything, but it does require less of the loyal spectators. I didn't have to question the eyesight of the referees or judgment of the coach. I could just sit and clap when everyone else did.

After the girls' game, as the boys' teams ran onto the floor to warm up, Detective Davis walked around the floor toward us.

"Ms. Hale." He nodded to me. He turned to MaryNell and offered her his hand. "I'm Sam Davis."

"MaryNell McLean," she responded. "Campbell said your daughter is one of the cheerleaders?"

"Yes, Julie Davis," he said, and gestured toward the clump of girls.

"My daughter, Melissa, is on the ball team. Number fourteen."

"Oh, yeah." He brightened. "She's a great player. Had a good game tonight."

They made parent small talk while I wished for the gym floor to open like the one in *It's a Wonderful Life.* I could quietly fall in, be swallowed, and everyone could go right on dancing.

"No more unexpected visitors, Ms. Hale?" he finally turned to me.

"No. No, everything's been quiet."

"Good. Well, nice to meet you, MaryNell."

"You, too, Sam."

"I'm sure I'll be seeing you at the games."

He went back to his daughter, who hugged him before he left. Oh, great. I needed someone to be angry at, and he was acting like the ideal man — good father, non-rebellious child, polite, not afraid of affection.

I waited until Melissa came out of the locker room so I could congratulate her on a good game, then left, too. I was going to take some ibuprofen and try to forget I knew myself. I'd made a fool of myself one too many times for one day.

Nothing seemed unusual at home, a couple more hang-up calls, no other messages. I should probably tell Detective Davis, but they were hang-up calls, not threats. I'd tell him the next time I saw him, I thought. I decided not to make a special call. I got a Coke from the refrigerator and held it against my forehead.

I seemed to hear every car that passed by, and they all seemed to be driving by slowly. I tried to turn off my imagination, but I couldn't seem to settle down. Eventually I started folding the pile of clean laundry sitting in front of my dryer. Sheets, towels, socks, T-shirts. So that's where all my underwear had gone. I put it all away, making several trips and feeling righteous.

I turned on the television for noise and

company, then turned it off again because it was annoying. I took the clean dishes out of the dishwasher and put them away. Then I loaded in the ones that had begun to accumulate in the sink.

When that was done, I started in on two week's worth of mail. Half of it could go directly in the trash without even being opened — loans; new credit-card applications, acceptance guaranteed; insurance; realtors wanting to sell my house; carpet cleaning. No, thanks, I have hardwood floors. Another 30 percent went into the trash after being opened — solicitations — great causes; I'd give if I could. Sales, loans, thank-you notes. Bills, bank statements, investment statements — I always save them, but what do I ever do with them? A letter from the physical therapist I met on a hiking tour of Ireland last spring. Never go on a hiking tour without a physical therapist. I wrote checks for the bills, found stamps, and placed them by the front door. I was still restless.

MaryNell called. "I have to say, Campbell. He's pretty cute. Maybe a little old for you, but not out of the ballpark." I didn't want to talk about it.

I changed the sheets on my bed and started a load of laundry. I turned the TV back on in time to see the news. After the headlines, after the first weather — rain, dropping temperatures, possible frozen precipitation of some kind depending on when the cold front arrived — a perky anchor began speaking in front of a photo of Rosie Layne.

"Rosie Layne and Jacqueline Miller, the adopted daughter of Jake and Hazel Miller, issued a joint statement today. Rosie Layne revealed that she is Jacqueline Miller's birth mother and that Jake Miller was, in fact, Jacqueline's biological father. Jacqueline said that she was delighted to have the opportunity to develop a relationship with her biological mother, particularly in the wake of the death of her adoptive mother, Hazel Miller. She said that Hazel and Jake had been very loving parents and she was sure they would want her and her son to enjoy this relationship.

"Rosie also said that she has chosen to reveal this information now because interest in Hazel's recent death has fueled speculation and led to the probability of the information becoming public. She contacted Jacqueline, and the two of them decided to forestall further speculation by making the information public. Dan?"

"That's a surprise, but maybe a good

beginning. We'll hope so. Bill says precipitation's on the way tomorrow. Are you going to need an umbrella or a snow shovel? We'll be back in a moment to let you know."

I sat down. I'd like to have felt good about what I'd done, to feel that I'd helped bring a mother and daughter together. If I were honest with myself, though, I'd have to admit that Rosie Layne had taken my meddling and made a courageous decision. And Jacqueline had been forgiving and mature enough to accept her. I had stirred things up more than I had done anything productive.

My phone rang. Stick had heard the news: "I hate to say it, but you were right, babe, at least about Rosie. But who murdered Hazel?" I told him I'd taken a new vow of meddling abstinence.

The call-waiting beeped. Mark: "Did you know this? Why didn't you let me know? What a story!" I refused to comment.

Another beep. MaryNell. "Did you hear? Did you know they were going to do that?"

Minutes later Randy called. He hadn't made the call he had promised after the show at the Bluebird, and I had decided he wasn't going to. But here he was. We discussed the news and made plans to have dinner in a couple of weeks. On a Monday, because he rarely played gigs on Monday nights.

Doug didn't get in touch. A half hour or so later, unsurprisingly, Detective Davis called. "Campbell. I guess you saw the news?"

"Yes, I did."

"Why do I think you had something to do with this?"

"I don't know. Maybe you always think of trouble when you think of me?"

"Not always."

"Well, maybe I did have something to do with it."

"I thought so."

I told him about the call from Rosie Layne and my visit with her. "I felt like a jerk," I ended.

"Why do you think she went public?" he asked.

"She probably thought I'd tell the papers, so she'd be better off telling the story first."

"Maybe. Or if you could figure it out, other people would, too. Maybe, just maybe, she figured it was time."

"I hope so." There was a long pause. "Your daughter seems very nice. She's lovely."

"Thanks. I'm proud of her. She looks like her mother, though, thank goodness."

Another pause. "I don't know any unawkward way to say this. Where is her mother?"

"Franklin."

"And you have custody? That's a little unusual."

"No. Joint custody. Her mother remarried a while back and moved to Franklin." Franklin was a small town in the next county to the south. "Julie didn't want to change schools, and I wanted her to live with me. But she spends a lot of time with her mother, too."

Where was I supposed to go from there? We talked for a few more minutes. I even called him Sam instead of Detective Davis. I hung up feeling oddly comforted.

The cold front stalled over Missouri and western Kentucky, so the bad weather held off. A gray cloud settled over the city, though, thick and ominous, not allowing us to forget what was just beyond that ridge of high pressure. My head hurt. I felt as if the clouds were a weight on my neck.

I tried to behave. I didn't like people yelling at me, and I still felt badly about Rosie Layne. The result of my meddling may have been a good thing, a family finding each other, but it was still meddling. It wasn't my place. And I was still a little jumpy when

I came home alone after dark.

I went to another ball game with MaryNell, but this time there was no grinning police officer across the floor or at the other end of the bleachers or at the concession stand. I went home even more depressed, even though McGavock had beaten Hunters Lane.

Work that week involved a flurry of families making Christmas and New Year's travel plans. Every year I get at least a dozen calls from people who want bargain trips during the week between Christmas and New Year's. As if nobody's ever thought of traveling then. That, of course, is one of the busiest times for travel. Everybody has Christmas and New Year's off — or at least some days around that time. All schools are out. Lots of manufacturers shut down for the week. College kids go home for Christmas; many families visit grandparents or vice versa. And pilots want time off, too.

Then, just when most of the space is sold, and hotels are booked solid for New Year's, bowl teams are announced. Every year around the first of December I'm scrambling to find airfare for UT fans to Phoenix or New Orleans or for Ole Miss fans to Atlanta.

So when, in the fall, somebody calls and

wants me to find a bargain trip to some-where *not too crowded* for the week between Christmas and New Year's, it takes all the courtesy and salesmanship I can muster not to say, "Stay home. No lines. No annoying strangers making noise in the room next door. No hours in uncomfortable chairs in any airport somewhere because your flight's been delayed by weather in Chicago or Detroit. Stay home!"

Instead, I start making calls, aware that it's useless but compelled to be able to say honestly that I tried. I call the wholesalers; I call the hotels directly; sometimes I beg. I look for alternate cities to fly into. I recheck the charters. I stay home.

Even through the preholiday work craze, I couldn't stop thinking about Hazel Miller. Hazel's life seemed so pathetic, such a waste of the vibrant, electric personality Gordy Adams had described. But for someone to end that life, to decide Hazel had no worth as a human being because of his — or her — own selfish purposes made me angry.

I started thinking again about who had what to gain. George Lewis had a job to lose and nothing to gain — unless he was working for someone else. He was inside the house, trusted. Who had more access to Hazel and her drugs? On the other hand, I didn't think Lewis would have used a drug that Hazel wasn't taking. It would have been too easy for him to have saved some pills from her prescribed stash. He probably picked up her prescriptions for her.

I knew the least about Jacqueline. As an anesthesiologist, she knew drugs and the limits of the human body. She, however, had a successful medical specialty practice and didn't have any visible vices or extravagances. Jacqueline was contained and controlled. Was that mature and secure, or was it a cover for resentment of an adoptive mother who had been emotionally absent? And what about her son, Jay? He was a loose cannon, a volatile explosive just waiting to be set off. And he wanted money to finance the career that would justify his identity.

I could not imagine what motive Franklin Polk might have, but he certainly wanted to be sure the sleeping dogs were allowed to lie undisturbed and to keep all the skeletons where he had hung them, neat and quiet in the backs of their mothballed closets. He was Jake's lawyer, and he made me curious.

I went back to my new friend Shana at the courthouse, but found no more information. No documents had been filed regarding Hazel's will. Maybe it was too soon, or maybe it was because of the murder investigation. Surely she'd had a will.

One night I went shopping with MaryNell, trying to get a start on Christmas. I bought a book on the World War II generation for Mr. Morgan and a construction set for one of my nephews. I kept noticing ties that would bring out the blue in the detective's eyes.

By Wednesday, I had been as good as I could stand. I decided to call George Lewis. I couldn't see what harm a few more questions could do.

"I really don't see the point of our discussing this," he said.

"There probably isn't any point," I agreed. "I'm just curious. Who was Hazel's attorney?"

Lewis named a well-known, established Nashville lawyer.

"Not Franklin Polk?"

"No. I know he was Jake's lawyer, but Hazel hated him. Maybe it was the way Jake's will was drawn up so she couldn't sell anything. She really didn't have a lot of money. I don't know. I just know something had happened before I knew her. Hazel had to be around Polk some. People associated him with Jake, and he was usually at any tribute kind of thing, but Hazel couldn't stand the man."

I called the office where Polk was still nominally a partner. His was the first of a long string of distinguished names, but I knew he no longer practiced. I pretended to be a reporter and asked if Mr. Polk were the attorney of record for Hazel Miller. The receptionist politely declined to give any information about who might or might not be clients of the firm.

I called my buddy Mark at *The Tennessean,* but he didn't know any more than I did. "I don't know what the bad blood was between Hazel and Polk," Mark said. "Polk drew up Jake's will that only let Hazel have a lifetime use of income from the estate. That would probably have been enough. Maybe his involvement with the adoption. Hazel had to know that Polk had known who Jacqueline was — and who her birth mother was — all along. Think how hard it must have been for Hazel, raising a daughter who was living evidence of Jake's unfaithfulness."

"I guess you're right."

"Campbell."

"Yes?"

"This is beginning to look too dangerous for you. I think it may be time for you to

246

give this up."

Not Mark, too.

CHAPTER FOURTEEN

The next morning started badly. I spilled coffee on my favorite sweater trying to juggle too many things getting out of the car at the office. I called Kenneth Elliott and amazingly found him in for the first time since I'd started researching the art museum in St. Louis.

"Hi, Kenneth."

"Campbell, hello." He sounded wary.

"What do you know about Franklin Polk?" I don't even know where that came from. I hadn't intended to ask. Franklin Polk was just nagging at my subconscious.

A pause. "Nothing. I've met him. I've probably sold his wife a painting or two. Why?"

"Oh, nothing. I don't know. About that museum in St. Louis . . ." I began.

"I can't talk right now," he said. "Just don't do anything. I'll be in touch."

I gave up. He didn't want to bother with

advising me on whether my senior citizens would enjoy visiting a museum in another city. They weren't likely ever to be clients of his. Neither was I, not a profitable client, at least. I'd just have to go ahead and make the decision myself.

The invoice printer went down. I wanted to go home and crawl back into bed. Then I remembered something a friend had told me while he was in AA. "Every day has twenty-four hours," he'd said. "If your day starts heading downhill, you can start over whenever you want. Live one day at a time, and whenever you decide, you can have a new day." I needed a new day.

I called the tech service, and they promised to have a technician on-site within two hours. I worked on the itinerary for the senior group trip until I felt satisfied with it and put the file away to review the next day. I helped a twenty-something plan a honeymoon that would make his bride the envy of her friends. I called Mark again at *The Tennessean* to see if he knew exactly what prescriptions Hazel had been taking and the name of the unexpected drug they'd found in her system. He didn't, but said he would ask around even though he really thought I should take his advice.

Stick called. "Hey, babe, I just got a weird

call from Gordy Adams. He wanted me to warn you —"

"Gordy Adams? What have I done to him?"

"Nothing. He just likes you. He doesn't know you very well, of course."

"Thanks, Stick. I may have to start my day over again."

"What?"

"Never mind. It's just been . . . Never mind. What did Gordy say?"

"He said he had heard, and he wouldn't say where he'd heard this, that you were stirring things up. He said some not entirely pleasant people said you needed to learn to leave things alone that didn't concern you and that it didn't seem to be idle conversation."

Then Franklin Polk called.

"Campbell Hale." It was more a command than a greeting.

"Yes, this is she."

"Miss Hale, you've been asking questions about my client's unfortunate death. Hazel Miller."

"Your client?"

"Yes, Mrs. Miller and I have been —" There was a pause. "— friends for many years. I have often assisted her as I did my dear friend Jake."

I didn't respond. I didn't know what to say.

"Jacqueline, Jay, and, of course, Miss Layne are all very distressed by the . . . events of the past few weeks. I know you would not wish to make things more difficult for them — or for your friend, Mr. Elliott — than they are already."

"Just what are you trying to say, Mr. Polk?"

"Miss Hale, you're a businesswoman. You know how . . . counterproductive it can be to make people angry unnecessarily. A lot of people in this town respect Jake Miller's memory and cared for his widow. They wouldn't want to see this become more . . . messy than it already is. Mr. Elliott, for example, Kenneth, could be hurt irreparably if his reputation were damaged by this. This is, after all, a very small town in many ways."

I was beginning to think that Mr. Polk's pauses communicated more than the words between them.

"Are you saying you represent Kenneth Elliott?"

"No, not at all. I'm just trying to appeal to your common sense."

"What is it you want from me, Mr. Polk?"

"I can be a very helpful person, Miss Hale. I think you would find that our being

251

friends would be very . . . helpful to your career and your future. And, of course, there's your friend, Mr. Elliott, Douglas. A very intelligent young man, very promising."

"I don't understand."

"I think you do, Miss Hale. You're very intelligent yourself. Just think about it. I can be a very good friend, or, well, just be . . . wise, Miss Hale."

I was speechless.

"Well, I'm sure we'll be in touch again, Miss Hale. Good-bye."

"Mr. Polk." I had nothing to lose.

"Yes, Miss Hale?"

"Just what did you and Jake Miller talk about the night he died? Was he telling you to arrange for Jackie to be taken care of? Was he about to leave Hazel for Rosie Layne? Was he firing you?"

He hung up.

Now my head was really hurting. I didn't want to start this day over; I just wanted it to end. I thought about calling Doug. I hadn't talked to him — or heard from him — lately, but I didn't want to listen to him tell me what was wrong with me. He'd hear about it soon enough, I was sure.

When I got home and opened my mail, my

day got worse. Someone had put a lien on my house. A lien on my house! I couldn't absorb it. I sat down and made myself start over. The letter came from one of the 150 or so lawyers in Franklin Polk's firm. The company that had come out to fix my air-conditioning last summer hadn't finished the job, so I hadn't paid them. They'd sent a bill; I'd written a letter. We'd talked. They'd said they really couldn't know if it was fixed until hot weather, so we were in a truce. So suddenly, for a $120 bill that I didn't think I should pay and nobody from the company seemed too upset about last week, there was a lien on my house! A lien placed by Franklin Polk's law firm! The letter said I would have to pay the amount in full plus a $150 legal fee to have it removed.

It was too late to call anybody today to find out what was going on. I picked up the phone to call Doug but hung up before I finished dialing. It was too late for him to do anything about it either. I'd wait until the morning and handle as much as I could myself before I talked to Doug.

I spent most of the next day straightening out the situation. The air-conditioning company's billing office hadn't known how it'd happened. They did occasionally file liens on homes for unpaid bills, but not unless the bill was a lot higher and a lot older than mine. Maxine confirmed the letter was from the law firm that represented the company. When I called, the attorney who had signed the letter said he got my information in a stack of other liens to be filed. He'd processed the liens. It was all pretty routine. He said he could only clear the lien when I paid. Maxine promised she'd get it straightened out, but she warned me that sometimes it could take weeks before a lien was removed. She apologized.

I couldn't prove it, but I knew Franklin Polk was behind it. I felt violated, targeted, powerless. And that made me mad.

For years I've had season tickets to TPAC's Broadway series. On play nights three friends and I meet for dinner before the performance. Pam is a friend from high school and a surgical nurse; the others, Betty and Melinda, work with Pam at Good Samaritan Hospital.

It was Friday night, a month since the last play, and we were meeting at South Street on Nineteenth just off Broadway before a revival of *Annie* at the Performing Arts Center. We ordered an asparagus and Monterey Jack Diver Dilla appetizer and started catching up. Pam asked if Doug was on or off these days, and I had to say off. She had started the master gardener course at Ellington Agricultural Center, and I offered my yard for her required volunteer community-service hours. "Just ask any of my neighbors. They'd all tell you what a service it would be to the community if someone would do something with my yard."

Conversation was difficult over the noise, but the food was tasty. South Street is an unpretentious beach restaurant landlocked in the middle of Nashville. The bar and narrow front room are open to the street in decent weather, drafty in winter, but the fireplace helps. The tiny back room is cramped and dim. Bright, whimsical murals disguise the cracks in the walls. The crab cakes are the best within five hundred miles, and you never know what the blue-plate special is going to be. The chef gets creative.

Betty and Melinda had not heard about my involvement with Hazel Miller's murder. I filled them in. "So you've probably talked to the murderer." Betty shivered. "Who done it, do you think?"

"No idea. Well, that's not true; too many ideas."

"Dr. Miller's really been stressed," Melinda offered.

"Dr. Miller?" I asked.

"Jackie, except we don't call her that around the hospital. It's Dr. Miller or Jacqueline. She really doesn't like to be called Jackie."

"I didn't know which hospital she worked at."

"I think she has privileges at two or three, but she's at Good Sam most of the time."

"I did a gallbladder with her yesterday," Pam offered. "She did fine, very professional, but yeah, she's been stressed. No joking around, no small talk. It's really been tough on her."

"Yeah," Betty added, "and she doesn't need any more stress. How long has it been since . . ."

They looked at each other, then away, embarrassed.

"What?" I demanded.

"It's common knowledge at the hospital." Melinda shrugged.

Pam explained. "Dr. Miller spent three months in rehab two years ago. The hospital doesn't like that kind of thing talked about."

"Maybe not, but it's pretty common," Betty returned.

They all watched my mouth drop. "Is that true?"

"Oh, yeah. Long days and nights, easy access to drugs, not as easy as it used to be, but still . . ."

"The hospital or the doctors' practices quietly pay for rehab when it happens. Part of the idea is that drug and alcohol problems will be dealt with better and more quickly if your job's not on the line, especially for a first-timer. If somebody knows or thinks you have a problem, they might be more likely to tell someone if they don't think it's going to destroy your whole career."

"And Jacqueline Miller?"

"Yeah. A couple of years ago. She had a pretty tough time, I heard."

"That's when her husband left, at least, when he left for good."

"I don't think it was the first time, for rehab, I mean," Betty added. "I heard something about it a long time ago, ten years, maybe?"

Melinda nodded. "You used to be on the state board that tracks that, didn't you, Pam?"

Pam nodded.

"Could I talk to them? Who oversees that?"

"The state health department, but they won't tell you anything. It's very confidential."

I sat back, trying to take it all in. I'd

thought Jackie was the stable one. Rosie Layne had neglected to mention Jackie's drug use when she talked about watching her daughter grow up in a household with substance abuse. Not that I blamed her for not talking to me about it. Maybe that's why Rosie had gone public about their relationship so quickly. She, they, might have hoped it would forestall more digging.

This changed everything. Even an anesthesiologist can need money when there's a drug habit to support. And maybe Jackie didn't have a drug habit, but she had once — or more than once. If she were innocent in all this, what a mess for a fragile person to have to deal with: the death of the only mother she had known, then finding out that death was murder; learning that her biological mother was someone she had seen and, to some extent, known all her life; looking out for her son, who seemed bent on self-destruction. Annie sang about her hard-knock life that night, but all I could think of was Jackie's.

That was before I got back to my car after the show and found my tires had been slit. I called AAA and George at AAAAuto, the only mechanic I would let touch my Spider. Two hours later I made it home. I didn't like feeling paranoid, but I was pretty sure somebody was out to get me.

Mark had left a message while I was out: Hazel's will had been read and released. I called him back in the morning.

"No surprises really," he said, "except for one that I thought you'd be interested in. Small legacies to the maid and George Lewis and a couple of friends, the house to Jay Miller, which could be quite a bit actually. Real estate in that area has really gone up."

"What about Jackie?" I demanded.

"I'm getting to that. The rest of her estate to Jackie, undetermined value, probably not much, maybe a net debt, but of course, the real value is in Jake's estate, which now goes to Jackie outright."

"We knew that already," I said impatiently.

"The rest of her estate except for the art collection. It goes to Kenneth Elliott."

"Kenneth Elliott?"

"Yep, except for the pieces that deal with Jake and his career, her collection of paintings and sculpture goes to Elliott. Her will encourages that a Jake Miller museum be established with the pieces directly relating to Jake's career."

"That would take a lot of money."

"Yes, and the will only suggests that. She had no money to fund it."

"Kenneth Elliott?"

"Oh, yeah, and Franklin Polk is the executor. You can read it in black and white tomorrow morning."

Why would Hazel name Franklin Polk — a man she reportedly hated, a man she had petitioned the court to have removed as executor of Jake's will decades before — to administer her own affairs after her death? It didn't make sense. And why had she left her art collection to Kenneth Elliott instead of her family?

I waited until ten, and then called Rosie Layne. Rosie answered; the dreaded Mrs. McKeever look-alike must have Saturday mornings off. "Miss Layne, you have no reason to talk to me, and I really don't want to cause you any more pain, but I just heard about Hazel Miller's will. Why would she have named Franklin Polk executor of her will? I thought she hated him."

Rosie sighed. She'd probably thought she was done with me. "Franklin Polk always handled Jake's dirty work. After Jake died, I considered trying to get Jacqueline back. I even started the paperwork to make a claim against the estate for Jackie's support. Franklin Polk came to see me. Quietly, politely, he made it clear that he would destroy me if I pursued it. Even if I won, and that would have been unlikely if he and Hazel were determined to fight it, he said he would make sure that I never worked in this town again. Not just singing, he said, 'You won't be able to get a job washing dishes, not in Nashville and probably not in the state.' Then he laughed. I didn't file the supporting documents, so the claim was denied."

People who don't know any better can listen to the down-home, good-buddy chatter — or, now, watch the back-slappin' and huggin' on the TNN cable broadcast — and think the Grand Ole Opry is just a bunch of country hicks sittin' around Nashville pickin' and grinnin'. Hardly. There are more lawyers in country music than guitar players, and the politics of who is asked to join the Opry or who gets a contract would put a lot of political machines to shame.

Rosie went on. "The next week I found ten thousand dollars in cash in my mailbox. No note. A month later, another ten thousand. I wasn't going to touch it, and I didn't spend any of it for a long time, but finally there was a day when I needed rent money, so I used some of it. As soon as I could I replaced it, put the twenty thousand in a bank account, and never touched it again. I was saving it for Jackie." She laughed.

"She's never needed it, of course, but it was a great comfort to me through the years, knowing that it was there for her. I imagined her leaving Hazel or being thrown out, having nowhere to go, and my going to her, saving her. Silly, but that bank account was going to be my proof that I had always loved her. Twenty thousand doesn't sound like that much, but it was there.

"Anyway, if Franklin Polk is involved, there's something to hide. Hazel had him removed as administrator of Jake's estate. I've always thought that had happened when she found out that Jackie was my daughter. She never spoke to me after that. Not that I cared."

I wanted to talk all this over with Sam, but for once, he didn't call. Not a word. I kept doing double takes when I saw plain, dark sedans, but no detective. I was beginning to miss that. Doug was out of town until sometime Monday. I didn't want to hear a sermon from him, but I needed to talk to someone. Stick, who had agreed to go out on a rare tour with a superstar, was in Las Vegas.

I picked up the Spider from George on Monday afternoon. "Maybe you could take a taxi the next time you're going to be

262

downtown late," he suggested. "Or Uber?"

The art-print cards arrived from the St. Louis museum, and I spent much of the first part of the week writing notes to clients about the trip, which was not very time-efficient. Handwriting notes was almost unheard of in this age of merge-mail and quick-print shops on every corner. But it seemed to fit this group, and I was counting on it to capture their attention and make them feel that they and their trip were special.

On Wednesday morning I called Kenneth Elliott at the gallery one more time. "Kenneth, this is Campbell Hale. I really need to talk to you about the Smith Logan museum. Please call me." I left office, mobile, and home numbers.

It was a card in the third box of prints that reminded me of the painting Doug and I had picked up for The Mockingbird Gallery. Four times on Wednesday afternoon I picked up a card with that painting on it, opened it, and began to write. Each time I became more and more sure that the painting had to be almost identical to Hazel's. Even if Kenneth had sold it to the museum, these cards had to have been printed long before Doug and I returned Hazel's paintings to the gallery. It had been my favorite of the paintings we had picked up; I suppose that's why I had noticed it more than the others. Before I sealed the last note, I stared at the painting for several minutes. The back of the card identified it as *Fleurs du Jour* by Henri de Suisse.

I called the Smith Logan museum and asked if all the paintings pictured on the cards I had ordered were currently on display. "I'm bringing a group there, and I had told them they would see these paintings."

"Yes," the curator assured me. "All of those paintings are on display now. We hung the Impressionist exhibit yesterday."

"You're sure? I'm especially interested in *Fleurs du Jour* by Henri de Suisse."

"Yes, quite sure. It's one of my favorites in this show. I know exactly where it's hanging."

I thanked her and hung up.

If Doug were in town, I could at least find out if both paintings were, indeed, by the same artist. Artists do often paint different versions of the same subject, but I could at least check that. I could be making something out of nothing. I was sure the list Kenneth had given Doug the day we went to Hazel's would be in a file in his office.

I called Doug's office. His personal assistant, Barbara, and I had become friends over the years. If she considered this information the least bit confidential, I had no hope of accessing the list, but it was worth a try.

Barbara was glad to help me out. She saw no reason why Doug would mind my seeing the list again. "I've already had to make copies for the police. What's your fax number?"

The list appeared within minutes. There were no titles, just artists' names and general descriptions. Second on the list was "de Suisse, Henri: Impressionist floral."

I retrieved one of the notes from the mail out-box, opened it, and rewrote the note on another card. I stuck the note with the de Suisse painting in my bag.

I was in line at the bank the next morning, Thursday, waiting to make the office deposit, when George Lewis walked in. Considering his attitude when I'd last seen him on Hazel's back lawn, I wasn't sure how he would react. He hadn't hung up on me when I called him, but I didn't think I was a favorite with him.

He stopped just inside the door, waiting for his eyes to adjust from the brightness outside. When he noticed me, he waved and came over to stand behind me in line.

"Miss Hale, how are you?"

"I'm well, and you?"

"I'm great, Miss Hale, just great." Lewis was ebullient; he was almost effervescent.

"You're a lot more cheerful than the last time I saw you," I observed.

"I am. I definitely am."

"May I ask why?"

"Miss Hale, can anyone keep you from asking questions anywhere, anytime, about anything?"

I was chastened. "I guess I deserve that."

"Yes, you do, but I don't mind telling you. I have a new job."

"That's great. What will you be doing?"

"I'll be a personal manager. I won't be carrying dinner trays to an alcoholic old woman who still thinks she owns this town." He named one of the biggest acts in country music. "I told you I had contacts. I'll finally get some real money."

"Well, congratulations. How did all this come about?"

Lewis laughed. "It really isn't who you know; it's what you know. You just use what you're given."

Cryptic. And all this time I'd thought it was a well-organized résumé, experience, and solid references that landed you a job.

266

"When do you start?"

"The first of the month. I'm taking a couple of weeks off first. It's been years since I've had a real vacation. I'm going to Saint Martin, get some sun, check out the nude beaches, hit the casinos. I should have called you. You're a travel agent, aren't you?"

Luckily, it was my turn at the window. Otherwise, I'd have probably had to listen to what a great deal he had found somewhere else. He was definitely not the same George Lewis who had been worrying about his next paycheck. And I didn't even want to think about him on clothing-optional beaches. He really must have had connections to land a job with someone on par with Alan Jackson, Vince Gill, and Kenny Chesney. But if Lewis were that well connected, why had he stayed with Hazel all those years? Had something changed since I had seen him last?

I finished my deposit and turned to leave. "Have a great trip."

"Thanks," Lewis acknowledged as he moved forward. "I need traveler's checks," I heard him announce to the teller, "hundreds."

I would have to see what my detective made of George Lewis's new prosperity. *My* detective?

Back at the office, I told Lee and Anna about Lewis and his sudden vacation.

"Who'd he have to blackmail for that?" Anna asked.

Now, that was a thought. I wondered what the maid's plans were.

That afternoon, when things slowed down at work, I thought about calling Hazel's house to see if the housekeeper was still there, but I didn't have the phone number. It was unlisted. I tried an Internet directory. No luck.

I wondered if Doug would give me the number. We hadn't talked lately. I really didn't want to ask him, but the worst he could do was say no. I called.

"I'm sorry, Campbell. Mr. Elliott is in a meeting. May I put you through to his voice mail?" She didn't sound as chummy as usual. I wondered if Doug had said something to her.

"No, thanks."

I decided to call Detective Davis, but I got voice mail there, too. I tried the gallery. Kenneth was out, but his assistant, a Vanderbilt art-major intern who looked fourteen going on twenty-five, answered.

"Miss Hale, of course, how may I help you?"

I had a story all ready, but I didn't need

it. She gave me the number efficiently, as if her only regret was that I hadn't asked for something that was more of a challenge.

The maid answered.

"My name is Campbell Hale. We met the afternoon Mrs. Miller died," I began to explain. "I was wondering if you're going to be looking for another job. I have a friend who is looking for someone reliable, and I thought of you." I was feeling pretty guilty, but at any given time I generally know five to ten people in need of an experienced housecleaner. If she really was looking for a job, I was pretty confident I could put her in touch with someone.

"No'm, Miz Hale. Thank you, but Mr. Lewis said he'd take care of me. I'll be here for a few more weeks takin' care of things, helpin' Miss Jackie get things straightened out and packed up, but then I'm goin' to work for Mr. Polk some, Mr. Franklin Polk. And I might retire before long. Mr. Lewis say I won't have to work if I don't want to, and I'm 'bout old enough to think that sounds pretty good."

At least Mr. Lewis was spreading his good fortune around.

I called Sam again and got his voice mail. This time I left my number. I would ask

him to come by for supper, and I wasn't
sure why, but the thought made me nervous.
I was a little relieved to put it off. A temporary reprieve.

Ten minutes later he called. "Campbell?"
He said it like my mother did when I was in
trouble. "What's up?"

"I wondered if you'd like to come by for
supper."

"Tonight?"

He was stalling. I've heard that tone
before. Why had I done this? I wanted to
hang up, but I was trapped, stuck there on
the phone.

"Actually, I was thinking tomorrow night."

"I'd like to. I'm sorry, but I can't. My
daughter's going to be home tomorrow
night. That's pretty rare on a Friday night
with a teenager, and I . . . really ought to be
home."

"Of course."

"Look, what about Saturday night?" he
countered.

"Ummh, sure, Saturday night's fine."

"Okay, good. What time?"

"Six, six thirty?"

"Can I bring something?"

"Nothing."

"Okay, thanks, I'll see you then."

"Okay, great," I agreed.

"Uh, is there anything you need to talk to me about before then?"

"No, no. I'll see you then."

"Okay, then, Saturday night."

Okay.

At least I didn't have to rush to the grocery store.

CHAPTER FIFTEEN

I still couldn't get the painting out of my head, and could think of only one way to find out for sure what I needed to know. I didn't want to approach Doug or, worse, Sam with some harebrained idea when my suspicions might have a very simple explanation. Lots of artists did similar studies of the same subject matter.

Just before lunch Friday, I convinced Lee to call The Mockingbird Gallery and ask for Kenneth. I didn't want him or the intern to recognize my voice. Kenneth wasn't there, and the intern didn't expect him to return before four thirty. I stuck the note in my pocket and grabbed my coat.

"I'm going to The Mockingbird Gallery, but don't tell anybody. I'll be back in, oh, no more than an hour, anyway."

I knew Kenneth had storage and a work-room at the back of the gallery. Surely I could find some way to get back there. If the paintings were still at the gallery and not hung in the display areas, that's where they had to be.

I made it to the gallery in fifteen minutes. It was only two, and the intern, Elizabeth, told me she didn't expect Kenneth for two and a half hours. Of course, he could come back earlier, so I didn't have much time to get in and out without him catching me. Luckily, a client followed me in.

"That's fine," I reassured Elizabeth. "I just need to look at something in Kenneth's workroom. It won't take a second. Go ahead, help the client."

Elizabeth seemed hesitant, but the client was looking impatient. She went with the client.

At the back of the gallery, a short hallway led from the last display room. To the left of this hallway was the office; to the right was a kitchen area. A door at the end of the hallway led to the workroom, where Kenneth kept paint, gold and silver leaf, varnishes, materials he might need to touch up a frame. In vertical compartments, paintings that were not on display were stored. That's where I expected to find the de Suisse.

I looked quickly through each bin that held paintings of approximately the right

273

size. None resembled the one I remembered or, in fact, any of the paintings we had taken that afternoon. I noticed that Kenneth not only stored touch-up materials; he had brushes of all sizes and textures, a large jumbled basket of oil and acrylic paints, easels. What appeared to be a large, oversize closet seemed to be carved out of one corner of the room. I tried the handle, but it was locked. Not too securely, though. I had learned to open locks like this one with a credit card as a child. After watching it done by private eyes on TV shows, my brother and I had practiced until we could do it in one swoop. I hadn't tried breaking and entering in a long time, but it was like riding a bike. It really does come back to you. I was inside, switching on the light in seconds.

Inside were more vertical bins. I found the painting almost immediately. The signature did indeed say *Henri de Suisse.* I pulled the card out of my pocket and compared it to the painting. It sure looked identical to me. On the back of the painting a copy of the letter of provenance was glued to the frame.

Fleurs du Jour by Henri de Suisse.

I shook my head and, as I did, noticed an unfinished painting on an easel at the back of the closet space. Hanging above the easel was the same painting, finished.

With my phone, I snapped a picture of the work in progress showing the original painting above it. I backed up as far as I could and took another of the de Suisse painting. I knew the quality would be awful, but at least there would be enough information that Kenneth couldn't dismiss it. My photos might not prove anything, but they would call for some serious explaining.

I slid the de Suisse painting back into its slot and exited the closet, trying to make sure I was leaving everything exactly as I had found it.

I was closing the door to the workroom behind me when I saw Kenneth heading through the gallery toward the hallway. In the relatively dim light, he didn't see me immediately. I knew I couldn't go back into the workroom and have him catch me there, but there was no place to hide. I stuffed the card back in my pocket and tried to look as if I were coming out of the kitchen area. I called his name just as he stepped into the hall.

"Kenneth, hi. I was just looking for the restroom."

He looked at me levelly, no smile, no expression, just wariness. "You didn't ask

Elizabeth where it was?" His eyes narrowed.

"She was busy with a client. Well, I'm off. See you later."

There was nothing natural about the way I acted. I just knew I had to get out of there. I wasn't going to improve the situation by staying and talking more. As I reached the door at the other side of the display room, he called my name.

"Campbell." I turned. "You didn't find the restroom back here."

"No, but I'm late. I've got to run."

And run I did. I jumped in the car and headed back to the office and didn't start breathing until I was halfway there.

I didn't know what to do.

Kenneth Elliott had in his gallery in Nashville, Tennessee, a painting that was at this very moment hanging in the Smith Logan Art Museum in St. Louis, Missouri.

I had to talk to someone, but who? I didn't know enough to want to start something that could potentially ruin Kenneth Elliott's career forever. Doug was Kenneth's brother, true, but I thought I could trust him. Despite our poor communication, I always had been able to trust him. Even if our relationship was fading. I still believed he was an honest man. Why had he picked now to be in Boston taking a deposition?

As soon as I got back to the office, I called and left messages on his home and office voice mails. "Doug, this is Campbell. I've got to talk to you as soon as you get back into town. Immediately. I . . . This is really serious. Please call me."

I decided to fix soup for the dinner with Sam. It's easy. Hard to mess up. It's good, but doesn't shout, "I'm trying to impress you." And I had more to concentrate on right now than exotic culinary skills. I started with a roast, cut in small pieces and seared, and added carrots, celery, garlic, lots of onion, potatoes, tomatoes. I sprinkled in thyme, basil, oregano, whatever smelled good. While that simmered, the aromas beginning to rise from the pot, I cleaned the house and put in laundry. I opened the windows to let in fresh air, but it got too cold, so I closed them. I went outside to see what last, straggling flowers and greenery I might find in the yard for the table and was just coming back inside when the phone rang.

"Campbell, this is Sam."

He's not coming.

"I'm not sure when I can make it tonight. Somebody found George Lewis this morning. He's dead. He was in a parking lot downtown, not far from Second Avenue, hit from behind as he was getting into his car, apparently. No witnesses, his wallet's gone, looks like robbery, but I don't like co-incidences. I'll call you later. Be real careful, okay?" Then the line went dead.

I felt a sudden chill.

George Lewis, dead. Had he been flashing around cash, talking big as he had been in the bank? Somebody could have followed him in the dark. But I agreed with Sam. Coincidences were suspicious. First Hazel, now George. I was suspicious and a little scared.

I turned the soup off. I couldn't just hang around the house all day wondering what was going on. I called MaryNell, and we set a time to meet at Opry Mills. I was already sipping coffee at the Starbucks kiosk when she arrived. My hands wouldn't stop shaking, and the caffeine probably wasn't helping.

"Shopping therapy? You need shopping therapy? You don't even like to shop."

"That's what makes it an emergency."

"So, what's up?"

I told her about George Lewis, about seeing him at the bank and his big plans. "The afternoon I went in Hazel's back drive and talked to him, he was digging in the flower beds back there, or at least he had been digging in dirt. I remember he stuffed something in his pocket when he saw me. I thought I was being overly suspicious at the time, but I think it could have been a prescription bottle."

"Was he burying it or digging it up?"

"I don't know."

"So you think he found the missing bottle and then he had money and a surprisingly good new job and now he's dead. Is your life insurance paid up?"

"MaryNell!"

"You know I've always wanted that Shaker side table of yours. Do you have it in your will that I get that? I don't want to have to fight with your family over it. I think it's so tacky when that happens."

"Do you have a point here?"

"The point here is that you're messing with somebody who kills people. If you don't want to be killed, stop it. Listen to Doug; listen to the detective. This is dangerous business, and it's not your business. Have you even told Sam about the slit tires and the lien?"

"Not yet. I'll tell him tonight." I hadn't told him about the tires or the lien. I hadn't seen him lately, and I didn't know what to make of it all anyway.

We wandered the mall for a couple of hours, not buying much of anything.

"So you've asked the detective over for dinner. That's good, not like you, but good. What are you having?"

I told her. Soup, homemade bread, salad, apple pie.

"That's just great. You'll remind him of his mother. Is that the emotional response you're going for?"

"I'm not going for anything. It's easy; it's good. I don't have to worry how it's going to turn out. Besides, I just want to talk to him. A lot's happened in the last few days."

"Phones? You both have phones?" MaryNell asked.

"Thank you for your encouragement. I just need to talk some things over with him."

"Right, right. Well, at least wear something red. It brightens you up. We can find you something new."

I escaped the mall without something new and red and went home to finish up supper. No messages, and Sam had made it clear that he didn't know when he would be here. About six I put the soup back on to simmer. The bread was ready; the salads were chilling; the table was set.

I tried to watch television.

"The tragic legacy of Jake Miller continues." Behind the weekend anchor played the tape of Sam, the homicide captain, and George Lewis at Hazel's front door on the night she died. "It was just a few weeks ago that George Lewis was assisting police who were investigating the mysterious death of his longtime employer, Hazel Miller, widow of country legend Jake Miller." Assisting? New spin since Lewis was dead. "This morning, his body was found beside his car in a downtown parking lot. We'll go to Kirsten at the scene. Kirsten, what can you tell us?"

On came a live satellite feed of Kirsten in a crowded parking lot.

"Dan, George Lewis's body was found early this morning by a parking-lot attendant who had come to collect parking fees from the lot behind me. He noticed the car's door was open, went around to investigate, and found Lewis's body. Police speculate that Lewis was getting into his car and was attacked from behind. The lot's crowded now with cars of people dining on Second Avenue and on Broadway, but this can be a pretty deserted area in the early morning hours."

"Kirsten, do the police think there's any connection between Lewis's death and

Hazel Miller's, or do they think it was a robbery?"

"Dan, it's just too early to say." The perky blond-framed face looked troubled. "They told us they're checking all leads, and they're appealing to anyone who passed along this street between midnight, when the attendant was here last, and six A.M., when the attendant returned, to contact Metro Police and tell them anything they might have seen."

"Thanks, Kirsten, I'm sure we'll have more on this at ten."

"That's right, Dan. We'll have the latest information then."

"It's been a big day in college football. We'll be right back with the scores and how today's results are likely to affect the BCS ratings and Tennessee's plans for New Year's after these messages."

The house felt chilly with the sun down. I lit the gas logs and went to find a sweater. I finally selected a red one and puttered, rechecking the salad plates, lighting candles, blowing them out, waiting to hear from Sam. I wondered just how much time the ex-wife had spent waiting.

It was after nine when he knocked, and he looked beat.

"Sorry. I came as soon as I could get free."

Everything about him was wrinkled.

"You want a glass of wine?"

"No, thanks. You have any tea?"

I fixed Sam a glass of iced tea and started putting food on the table. "What happened?"

"We think sometime between two and six, probably between two and four, Lewis went to his car." Sam shrugged out of his jacket and laid it over the back of the couch. A pager, handcuffs, and his badge were clipped to his belt. He checked the safety on his gun and returned it to the holster on his belt. It was a routine, as thorough as it was automatic. Sam continued, "Somebody came up behind him, hit him hard enough to knock him out, or at least temporarily incapacitate him, then hit him a second time to kill him. That's what we think, anyway. His wallet is missing. Usually with a robbery, you find the wallet within a couple of blocks. Nothing. We've looked at every cigarette butt, every ticket stub, every gum wrapper within a quarter mile in every direction. I'm here to tell you there's a lot of trash in this town."

"So do you think it was robbery?"

"I don't know. He was robbed, but was that the reason or was it a cover? There was no sign that Lewis resisted, no sign that he even knew he was in danger. It's a little unusual for the victim to be killed in a simple robbery. But then again, you never know what some guy spaced out on whatever is going to do. Junkies don't think clearly."

"What about Jay Miller? Was he playing downtown last night?"

"We're checking. He says he was at a studio out in Mount Juliet working a session. They were at it pretty late, finished about three. He went straight home and to bed. One of his housemates is in his band. His story is the same, says they left Mount Juliet about the same time, got to their house in the Melrose area about the same time."

I started coffee, got everything on the table, and said, "I have a few things to tell you." He didn't look cheered up by that. I decided food might help.

The soup smelled great as I ladled it into the bowls. Sam closed his eyes and inhaled. That was a good sign.

"What have you been up to while I've been picking up trash?" he asked.

"Well," I began. I told him about Lewis in the bank, about Anna's joking suggestion that he might be blackmailing someone. Sam ate like a man who was hungry and tired. I told him about the lien and about the slit tires on the Spider. He scowled. I told him about my information that Jacqueline had had a drug problem and spent time in rehab. He raised his eyebrow at that; hospitals keep that kind of thing very quiet.

He took a long drink of tea. "Jacqueline would have known what medications her mother was taking, and she would have been smart enough to make sure she used drugs Hazel was already taking. This soup is great, by the way. And the bread. You make it?"

I nodded.

"It's really good." He looked impressed. Tired, but impressed. "But we'll do some more checking on her statement, where she was that afternoon. She was in the hospital, and most of the time she said she was in surgery. It was a high-risk surgery, and she was in and out of the OR through the whole thing. It might have been possible to make it out to Hazel's; I don't know. I would think someone would have seen her coming or going, but that doesn't mean they would have thought anything about it. Who are your sources, anyway? How do you find out these things?"

I tried to look modest, but I didn't tell. "Oh, and the maid! She said Mr. Lewis said he would take care of her, that she would work for Franklin Polk, but if she didn't want to work, she wouldn't have to. That's unusually generous, don't you think?"

At that point, he got up, went over to his jacket, and grabbed his notebook. This was not going to be a nice, relaxed evening. I was trying to decide if I should tell him about the painting in Kenneth Elliott's back room. I thought about getting the photos from my bedroom, but I didn't. I really wanted to talk to Doug first. There had to be some legitimate explanation.

"When did you talk to the maid?"

I told him.

He pulled his phone out of his pocket and hit a number. "Tom. This is Davis. Check out the maid. She may still be at the Miller house. If not, check with Franklin Polk. I don't care if you do interrupt his weekend. She was expecting to start work there when she was through at the Millers'. If Lewis's murder is connected to Hazel Miller's, she might be at risk, too. Okay. Thanks."

He returned to the table, started to say something, then stopped.

"What?" I asked.

He looked at me, then away for a moment. "It's probably nothing. Somebody in Fraud thinks he may be onto something that might connect. Probably not. You mentioned apple pie?"

I cut the pie and served pieces on dessert plates. "I forgot. When I talked to Lewis in Hazel's backyard, he stuck something in his pocket that I thought he might have been trying to hide. Maybe something like a medicine bottle? Ice cream?"

He gave that some thought. "No, I don't think so. Just pie."

"Coffee?"

"Yes, but I'll get it."

He poured the coffee for both of us and brought it to the table. He took a bite of pie and closed his eyes again. Either he really liked it, or he was so tired he was about to fall asleep.

"That is delicious. Do you cook a lot?"

"Not a lot. I like to cook; it's just usually easier to fix a sandwich or a salad or microwave a Lean Cuisine. What about you?" I asked.

"Me?"

"Yeah. Do you cook?"

"Enough to keep Julie from going hungry. Basic stuff. We eat a lot of raw vegetables." He grinned. "Nutritious, and if you don't cook 'em, you can't mess 'em up. I guess I cook badly enough that Julie was motivated to learn to cook early. She's a much better cook than I am."

"My friend MaryNell's daughter says she's a nice kid."

He nodded. "I've spent enough time around courtrooms to know that parents don't always know what's going on even if they try, but yeah, she is a nice kid. Smart, together." He looked up and into my eyes. "I'm proud of her. I don't mean I'm proud of myself because of her. I'm proud of her, of the woman she is becoming."

I smiled and thought, not for the first time, that I could have been a mother by now if I'd made some different choices. It wasn't too late, but it was getting there. "Sounds to me like you're a lucky man."

He nodded again. The silence stretched. His phone rang.

"Davis. Okay. Good. You got the sister's number and address? Okay." He hung up. "The maid's okay. She was at the Miller house, but she's going to stay with a sister." He looked away. "Look, don't repeat that. Not to, well, not to anybody. I don't think you've murdered two people in the last few weeks. I'm not too sure about anybody else."

"Sure."

"I, uh, this was great, and I'm sorry that I was so late, but I think I'd better head on home," Sam said.

"Sure. I know you must be tired."

"Yeah, I am. Uh, thanks for supper. It was nice. Would you like to try it again sometime when I'm not in the middle of a murder?" He checked his gun, a reflex, then collected his holster and jacket. Armed again, he was ready to go.

"Yeah. That would be nice."

He started out but turned back. "Listen, I was serious when I told you to be careful. Don't open your door to a stranger. Don't go out at night by yourself. Call your friend. Be real careful."

CHAPTER SIXTEEN

This bottle won't judge me; it won't criticize;
It listens to whatever I say.
This bottle won't leave me; it won't break
   my heart;
It waits for me here every day.

You say that you love me;
I know that it's true.
We've been through so much for so long.
You've been here beside me;
You've tried hard to save me;
You're the best friend that I've ever known
Except for this bottle right here.
                        — Jake Miller,
   "The Best Friend That I've Ever Known"

Monday morning I woke to rain on the
skylight, a wonderful sound if only I could
stay in bed an extra hour or so. Unfortu-
nately, I had to go to work. I reminded
myself to be grateful that I had a job I had

to get out of bed for. It almost worked.

Nashville is a bad town for driving, and bad weather seems to bring out the aggression in us. We drive too fast and too close. I try to leave a little extra space when it rains, but invariably someone cuts in front of me, signaling only after he's changed lanes to announce his accomplishment instead of his intent and halving the space. That often makes the twenty-five-minute drive twice as long and twice as stressful. So I got to work tense and late with too many messages already in my voice mail.

It was going to be a long day. I called Doug's office. He was back but "in a meeting," so I left a message on his voice mail: "Why would Hazel Miller leave her art collection to Kenneth?" I worked through lunch, wolfing a sandwich at my desk, a pizza sub that Anna brought me when she went out. I made time to call the state health department board's office. Yes, a Ms. McMillan admitted, her office did oversee health-care workers who had had treatment for substance abuse problems, and no, she could not give me any information on any physician. That information was confidential. Then I had to finalize my group itinerary and get it to the printer. And I wanted to leave work in time to go home and change before I met Randy at Jimmy Kelly's at seven.

Doug finally called. "It doesn't matter why Hazel left Kenneth her art collection, not that there's much of it. Some people leave their estates to pets. And I can't talk about it to you anyway because Kenneth's my client."

Brick wall. "Didn't you tell me that Kenneth doesn't paint anymore?"

"Far as I know, but if he does, it's none of your business." Doug sounded mad.

So I didn't even go into the whole painting-in-the-closet thing.

I double-checked the hotels where I had blocked space for the art tour, driving times, and menus. I went ahead and included the Smith Logan museum and St. Louis overnight in the itinerary. I decided it might not be a great idea to try to consult with Kenneth Elliott on that museum anymore.

The house was chilly when I got home; the temperature was definitely dropping. I lit the gas logs in the fireplace and stood in front of it to warm up. I was supposed to meet Randy at Jimmy Kelly's in an hour, and I wanted to change, wash my face, put on fresh makeup. I wished I had time for a shower, but then my hair would go limp, and I'd have to do something with it. I didn't have time for that.

In the bathroom, I pulled my hair up into an elastic band and washed my face. The phone rang, but the water was running, so I didn't hear it in time to catch it. No message: an uncommitted caller. Caller ID showed a number I didn't recognize, but no name. I put hot rollers in my hair while I applied makeup. It didn't take long: concealer, blush, a little eye shadow and mascara. I'm blond. If I don't wear mascara I look like I have no eyelashes. But I didn't have the time to do much else with my makeup — or my hair, for that matter. I felt thrown together.

I pulled the curlers out and changed clothes. I thought about a dress, but decided on pants because of the possible snow. Gray slacks, the new gray silk blouse I had just bought at Off 5th, and a pink cashmere sweater. I looked in the mirror. Not bad. Pink's a good color for my skin. I brushed my hair, found my long, navy wool coat, and headed out. Gloves, I always forget gloves. I went back to the closet and found them. I turned off the gas logs, checked to make sure all the doors were locked, and turned on all the outside lights.

Outside, I could tell that it had gotten

colder, even in the short time I'd been home. I turned on the car radio to hear a weather report. For once, nothing but music, Gary Lewis & the Playboys. I sang along and cranked up the heat.

I took I-40 to the Church Street exit, then drove out past Baptist Hospital to Elliston Place and right on Louise. It was cold and I was driving alone, so I decided to valet park. Randy was waiting just inside the door.

"Hey. I'm glad you're here." He leaned over and kissed me lightly on the cheek. Nice. "It'll just be a few minutes. Want something to drink?"

We went into the bar, dark with Southeastern Conference school banners all around, and I had a club soda with lemon and lime. I love Jimmy Kelly's in the winter. It's always just a little overheated, probably because it's an old house and not terribly well insulated. If you sit by a window on a cold night, you can tell. But the atmosphere is warm and comfortable. The food — steaks are the specialty — and service are wonderful but unpretentious. I was thinking of the smaller filet or rib eye and salad with the house Roquefort dressing. I'd been thinking of it all day.

When our table was ready, we were seated in the front room near the fireplace, just where I like to sit. The rooms are small, and so are the tables. The lights are dim and forgiving, hiding your imperfections as well as those of the old house with its slightly uneven floors and wide wooden banister. It's a place to talk and linger. I felt more relaxed than I had in weeks. Our waiter, a charming older man in a crisply starched white jacket, knew Randy and treated him like a nephew. He brought out Jimmy Kelly's signature hot corn cakes with butter. They're addictive. I was disciplined, pacing myself for what was to come.

Maybe it was the comfort food; maybe it was the warm fire on a cold night. Maybe it was a really nice man who seemed to like being with me, but I had a great time. It was the first time I'd been with Randy without Stick. We talked and laughed, getting to know each other, and it seemed that the food came too soon. We dawdled over coffee; then, finally, it was getting late and there was no more reason to stay.

Randy helped me into my coat and kept his arm around my shoulders as we walked down the short brick walk and waited for my car. It was sleeting.

"I could follow you home," he offered.

I wasn't sure exactly what he was offering. "Thanks. That's sweet, but I'll be fine."

"Be careful. I'll call to make sure you get home, okay?" He tipped the valet, then, again, kissed my cheek, and closed my car door. I drove away smiling to myself. I'd had a wonderful time with a wonderful man. Then I frowned. So why was I thinking about a lanky, annoying detective, wondering what he was doing tonight?

CHAPTER SEVENTEEN

As I drove away from Jimmy Kelly's, a car pulled out a few spaces back and was behind me on Louise. It was still with me as I turned left onto Church. It wouldn't have been the first time someone had been following me, but I decided I really did have to stop all this amateur detecting. I was beginning to get paranoid. Then I remembered an old saying from the sixties: just because you're paranoid doesn't mean they're not out to get you.

I hadn't gotten to the interstate when my cell phone rang.

"Miss Hale?"

"Yes. Who is this?"

"Franklin Polk."

Franklin Polk? How had he gotten my cell-phone number?

"You've been asking a lot of questions, Miss Hale. Questions that have nothing to do with you, of course, but they're inconvenient for some good people. Let's meet. I think I can explain things to your satisfaction. Come to my house."

I stammered. "I'd like to talk to you, of course, but it's late and the roads are bad tonight." If he was willing to talk, maybe I could figure some things out now. "If Hazel Miller resented you so badly, why did she choose you to be the executor of her estate?"

"Miss Hale."

"And was she in the car with Jake in Louisville?"

"I'm not going to talk with you about anything on the phone. I'm leaving town in the morning," he said. "I'm afraid this is it. If you have any legitimate interest in this, you can come now. Otherwise, I'd advise you to desist. One of my clients has already mentioned a suit for harassment."

Harassment? Who were his clients? I thought he was retired. But if he was leaving town, this might be my only chance for some real answers. "Okay. I'm on my way."

He gave an address and hung up.

I really wanted to be home. The roads were beginning to get slick, and it was already late. I swallowed my fear and took the I-65 fork to the south. It was, after all, a nice, very upscale neighborhood. I wished I had the museum brochure or the note card with me. I'd left them all at home.

I thought of Doug. Kenneth was his brother, after all. And Doug was my friend.

I tried Doug's home number, but there was no answer. I had Doug's cell-phone number in my phone address book, but I didn't have it memorized. The roads were too slick for me to look down at the display, and I didn't think it wise to pull over to the side of a highway in this weather, so I left a message. Of course, that wouldn't help much if Doug was already asleep or back in Boston or just out for the night.

"Doug, this is Campbell. I know it's late, but I really need to talk to you. I won't ask questions; I'll just tell you some things I think you need to know. It's eleven. If you get this message in the next fifteen minutes, would you call me?" I knew he had my cell number, but I left the number anyway. "I'm on my way to Franklin Polk's house — at his request." I gave the address on Otter Creek Road. "Thanks."

The road was icy. My Spider is usually pretty good in bad weather, but I could feel my tires slip occasionally. The contented glow in which I had left Jimmy Kelly's was fading quickly. I wanted to be home and warm. And safe.

Otter Creek Road curves and hugs a steep

hill above Radnor Lake, a small lake and park between Granny White Pike and Franklin Road south of downtown. I drove out I-65 to the Harding Place exit and went right to Franklin Road. A couple of miles south, I turned right onto Otter Creek Road and began to climb.

I was near the address Polk had given me, but it was hard to see. The windows of the houses were all dark, and the houses were set back from the road in treed lots. Great. The constant clicking sound of the sleet hitting my windows punctuated the darkness. I drove slowly, looking for the right number, but not all the addresses were marked at the street. Small numbers on mailboxes were virtually invisible in the dark, the icy glare of sleet blurring them further. The car was finally beginning to get warm, and the windows were fogging.

The road was too narrow to turn around, and the grade was steep. When I tried to pull to the side a little to orient myself, my headlights hit a bronze plaque on the side of a stone mailbox several yards in front of me. Polk.

From behind me and uphill, I heard an engine. Suddenly headlights filled my car and reflected in my rearview mirror. I couldn't see a thing. The guy must have his lights on bright; surely he could see me now.

The car still came toward me in the middle of the narrow road. I tried to wipe from the inside, but the back window was fogged, too. I decided the driver either couldn't or wasn't going to stop in time, so I started downhill, the gears grinding as I shifted, too nervous to do it smoothly. I tried to watch the icy road and the idiot in my mirror at the same time. I was trying to drive carefully on the ice, but he seemed to be coming faster. I speeded up as much as I thought I should under the circumstances, but he kept coming, accelerating faster than I was, gaining on me.

The Spider was slipping. Black ice. Legendary around here because you couldn't distinguish it until you started sliding. Like now. Then a dry patch. Traction. For a minute.

I thought about what my mother would say. I shouldn't have been out on a night like this. I shouldn't have been out here by myself. I shouldn't have been out where no one knew where I was except an idiot out-of-control driver, a guy who had rudely demanded my presence this late on a night with horrible weather, and an answering machine whose owner was probably asleep.

The car kept coming, and I was driving

faster and faster, the Spider slipping and sliding around the icy curves. I was proud of her, but I was terrified. How old were my tires? I should have checked the tread before this kind of weather started. Then I remembered. They were almost brand-new. I'd had them replaced after they were slit. That made me feel better for about half a second. Maybe my slit tires hadn't been random vandalism.

Trees loomed briefly in my line of vision at the edge of the shoulderless road. I looked for a driveway I could swing into and get out of the guy's way, but the few I saw turned too sharply for me to make at this speed.

The car edged to the left, and I thought, *Great, it's going to pass me. I don't know how, but it's going to pass me.* I pulled as far as I could to the right to give him as much room as possible, but I couldn't get too close to the edge at this speed and with these curves.

Then I realized the idiot wasn't trying to pass me. And he wasn't out of control. He was getting closer and trying to run me off the road, down the side of the hill and into the trees and the lake beyond. Was he trying to kill me? He? She? Who was it?

The sound of the engine penetrated my fear, loud and angry. Why was someone trying to run me off the road? And how could I keep him — her? — from succeeding? Where was that detective who had been around so much lately?

I pulled back to the middle of the road. I tried to speed up, but he kept coming, trying to force me to the right. Then he hit me. He hit my left rear bumper! The Spider bumped and skidded to the right. I got her back under control inches from a tree and pulled back to the middle of the road. Then he hit me again. I skidded to the right again. A tire spun in mud, but I managed to pull back. I tried going faster, but I was skidding all over the road, sliding across patches of ice. My cell phone started ringing, but there was no way I could answer it.

How high was this hill anyway? I was just thinking there couldn't be too much farther to go before the road leveled out when I saw headlights approaching. I was meeting a car, snow chains on, carefully navigating the steep incline. The driver behind me backed off. I kept moving to the bottom of the hill, but he wasn't following me anymore. I turned right on Granny White, toward town and people.

I was shaking now but afraid to stop, continuously checking my mirrors to see if anyone was following me. No sign of him.

The streets were deserted — except for the cars that had slid into ditches.

I was afraid to go home. Afraid whoever it was knew where I lived and wasn't behind me now because he was already on his way there. Waiting for me.

I dreaded calling Detective Davis. He would say he'd told me to stay out of this. So I went to MaryNell's.

"Campbell! What's wrong? What are you doing out on a night like this?"

I was still shaking. I couldn't answer.

"Well, get in here! Come on. I'll fix us some hot tea."

I couldn't argue with that.

MaryNell's husband, Richard, was stretched out on the couch watching basketball. Richard waved as we passed through.

In the kitchen, MaryNell put water on to boil, pulled mugs from a cabinet and tea bags from a glass container. "Are you okay?" she asked. "You're not okay. I can see that for myself. What happened?"

I took a deep, shuddering breath. "This sounds crazy." I stopped. It did sound crazy. "I think someone just tried to kill me."

MaryNell splashed hot water as she filled the mugs, causing the gas flame on the stove to flare up. She turned to me. "What are you talking about? What happened?"

I tried to tell her. I started with Franklin Polk's call. I watched her face change from alarm to indulgence. "Campbell, cars are running, sliding off the road all over town. I'd be the first to tell you to be more careful, but, honey! The roads have turned to ice in the last couple of hours. I know it must have been awful, but the guy probably couldn't help it."

"MaryNell, the guy hit me! He wasn't even trying to miss me or slow down or go around me. He wanted me to go off the side of that hill!" It was beginning to sound foolish even to me. But I was sure I was right. I was sure he had driven toward me when he could have gone around me. I was positive. I thought.

"Here. Drink this. You'll feel better. Put some honey in it."

Was I crazy? Was I imagining people were trying to kill me now? I drank my tea, scalding my tongue so it didn't matter how it tasted. But it brought me back to reality. People didn't kill people in my world, did they? People had accidents and messed up their cars, especially on nights like tonight. Somewhere some poor guy was probably telling his wife about how his brakes wouldn't work and he'd almost hit some car, how he'd tried to steer in the other direction but he'd just kept sliding toward the car, relieved at the near miss. . . .

"MaryNell, I couldn't have imagined it!" Was I trying to convince MaryNell or myself?

I heard Richard groan as the game ended; then SportsCenter came on.

"Of course not," she said, soothing me, "but have you heard the news tonight? The police can't even get to the wrecks where people are injured, there are so many of them. Schools are already closed tomorrow. I know you had to be terrified, but you're okay now. And you're not going back out. You'll stay here tonight."

I started to protest, but I didn't have the strength. Besides, I didn't want to go home alone.

"Okay."

"Good. I'll fix you another cup of tea." She took my mug back to the counter. "And we've got pecan pie left from supper. What were you doing out in the first place?"

"Randy. I had dinner with Randy." Dinner at Jimmy Kelly's seemed years ago.

"Stick's friend? The songwriter?" She turned to look.

I nodded.

"So?" She came back to the table with

more tea and two plates of pie. "Did you have a good time? Before the ice thing, I mean? You realize this is two dates — with two different men — in one week."

"No. Sam wasn't a date." But I had had a good time, and Doug didn't seem to be coming around anymore. I told her about it, trying to remember that nice warm feeling I'd had when I left Randy — before the idiot on the hill. Trying not to believe someone wanted me dead.

CHAPTER EIGHTEEN

The next morning I went home to take a shower and change clothes before going to work. The salt and brine trucks had been out, and the main roads weren't too bad. With schools closed, there would be less traffic, except around the malls, and that would help. Why is it when the roads are too dangerous for schools to be open the malls are always crowded?

There was no message from Doug. No message from Franklin Polk.

My first call was to Polk. His housekeeper answered.

"I'm sorry. Mista Polk is not at home. May I take a message?" He'd told me he was leaving town. So much for finding out whatever he might have told me. Unless he hadn't intended to tell me anything. Unless his call had just been the bait to get me out on that road. He had been the only one who knew I was there. I shook my head, water

308

flying from my wet hair.

On the drive in to work, I debated calling Detective Davis. MaryNell was my friend. If she hadn't believed me, I couldn't imagine Sam Davis would. He would preach at me to mind my own business, and I wouldn't even get tea and pecan pie.

"You made it!" Lee said as I entered the office.

"Yeah. Did you have any trouble?" No one else was there yet, and I was debating whether to call the others and tell them not to come. Then again, if people were home without much to do, they'd think about tropical vacations and call. On days like this, the idea of getting out of town sounded even better. I'd wait and see how it went.

Lee and I swapped ice stories, and I told him about my hillside adventure of the night before. He sided with MaryNell with more patronizing and less sympathy. "The wonder is that either of you made it down off that hill last night." He shook his head. "It was a mess."

"Yeah, I guess." But he hadn't been there.

I still hadn't been able to talk to Doug about the paintings. I couldn't believe Kenneth could be a murderer, but I didn't believe he was a forger, either. Doug was in a meeting when I called, but he called back and agreed to meet me for lunch. "I'll come there," he said. "No need in both of us being on the road. I'll meet you at Pancake Pantry."

Doug's face was set and hard when he walked through the door. I was already seated. Not much of a wait today. With the weather so bad, people tended to stay in if they could, eat at their desks.

"What is it you're trying to do?" he asked. "And what's your point? Do you even have a point, or do you just get off on making trouble?"

I had never seen Doug this angry. Whatever I'd said about his not expressing emotion I'd have to take back. He sure was expressing it now, and it wasn't fun. But then I started to get mad, too.

"I could have just told this to the police, you know, or Mark. I came to you because I'm trying *not* to make trouble, because I *thought* we were friends, and I should talk to you."

Face-off. Two angry, red faces.

"One decaf, one regular?" The waitress broke the hard silence.

Doug nodded.

"Please," I said, "and I'm ready to order." The waitress's smile was genuinely bright.

Doug and I glared at each other like two gunfighters in the middle of a dusty street.

"Okay. What is it?" Doug asked as she walked away.

"I thought you'd said Kenneth gave up painting years ago."

"Yeah. So what?"

"Well, I don't think so." I told him about the locked room at the back of the gallery. About the half-copied painting.

"So what?" I could tell Doug was surprised, but he still didn't get it.

"There's more. One of the paintings we took from Hazel's house is in a museum in St. Louis."

Doug made a disgusted sound. Then he turned patronizing and sarcastic. "Painters learn by copying great artists; it's a discipline thing. There's nothing in that. And your painting in your little museum is probably just another study of the same subject — if it's even like the one at Hazel's at all. Or Ken could have sold it to them. He's an art dealer, you know. It's what he does."

I nodded, too mad to speak. I pulled out the note card and the list of Hazel's paintings I'd gotten from his office. "They didn't *just* buy this painting." I stabbed the card with my finger and pushed it across the table to Doug. "It's been hanging on their wall, and you can already buy these nice cards." I flipped it over to show the title and artist's name. "You tell me if it's *even like* the one at Hazel's!"

I watched Doug and caught the moment he wavered. His eyes moved to the list from his office. He shook his head. "This doesn't prove a thing." The lawyer face was back, a cool, hard mask sliding over the anger, over any doubt.

"Fine. I tried." I drank half the coffee in one gulp and got up. I found the waitress, asked for my lunch to go, paid, and left. Outside, I passed the window by the table where Doug still sat. I looked away.

The cold air felt good against my face on the short walk back to the office.

"Anna called again. Said she still hadn't been able to get down her hill. I told her I'd call her back when I checked with you, but she should probably stay home. The phone hasn't rung except for her."

"Yeah." I nodded. "That's fine. Have you heard from Martha?"

"Not yet."

I called her. No answer at home. Already on her way, stuck in traffic, or off in a ditch. I tried her cell phone.

"I'm on my way," she said, but she sounded stressed.

"Where are you?"

"Not far from home. It's really slow going."

"If you want to, just go home. If you can find a place to turn around."

"You sure?" I could hear the relief in her voice.

"Yeah, nothing's going on here. Lee's here. I'm here. Nobody's calling."

"That would be great."

"Do you have any payment deadlines, anything that has to be done today?" I heard a horn. Then a crunch. "Was that you?"

"No. Thank goodness. This guy started sliding, and he just kept going, right into a guardrail. Slow motion." She shifted mental gears. "No, no deadlines until Monday. Mrs. Turner might call. If she does, just call me, and I'll call her back."

"Okay. Well, we'll see you tomorrow. Be careful."

"You, too. Thanks, Campbell."

Lee and I fielded the few calls and caught up on paperwork. I organized my files on current projects and straightened my desk. I went back through the senior-trip itinerary and readied the last of the notes, and when the mail carrier came by, I offered her a cup of coffee to warm up. This was a walking

313

route, and it couldn't be fun today.

Traffic and weather were the news on the radio: wrecks, side streets blocked by cars, and trucks sideways. More freezing rain was due this evening. The sky never lightened up; it stayed charcoal gray all day.

I wondered what Doug had done after I left. Had he called Kenneth?

By three thirty, Lee and I were caught up and staring out the door at the lights that came on automatically, already punctuating the gray sky.

"Why don't you go on home?" I said to Lee.

"I hate to leave you here alone." He meant it, but he was thinking about the roads.

"It's fine. I'll leave early myself. I'll just wait until four at least."

"You're sure?"

"Yeah. Go. There's no point in both of us sitting here."

"You've got your cell phone in case you have any trouble getting home?"

I nodded. "Yeah, I'll be fine."

It seemed much later than it was. "Why don't you lock the door? You could unlock it if a client you know comes." We did that sometimes if one of us was here alone late, after the businesses around us were closed.

I shrugged. "I might. But I'll be fine."

Lee had his stuff together to go in seconds. "If you're sure."

"I'll be fine. Go."

He went.

The office was silent except for the quiet hum of the fluorescent lights and the printer.

I jumped when the phone rang. "Get Out of Town. This is Campbell. May I help you?"

"You're still there?" MaryNell. "Why don't you come back and spend the night again tonight? I've made chili."

"That sounds good, but no, thanks. I'm just going to go home and turn on the fire. Drink hot chocolate maybe."

"You should leave before the ice moves in again."

"Yeah, I'll probably close up in a few minutes. It's dead here. Been that way all day."

"Well, do call me if you have any trouble."

I laughed. "Yeah, what will you do?" MaryNell's husband handled the vehicles. Division of labor.

"I'll send Richard. And call me when you get home so I don't worry."

The phone rang again, but no one spoke when I answered. I hung up. Bad weather does funny things to Nashville phones. It rang again immediately. My mom.

"There's more bad weather moving in," she said. "You ought to go home early if you can."

"Yes, ma'am. I'll go soon."

"Well, be careful. Call if you need us."

Another ring. Lee and I had sat there all day; now the phone was ringing off the hook.

"Get Out of Town. This is Campbell. May I help you?"

"I'm ready to get out of town. You got a nice, warm, sandy beach somewhere?"

It was Sam.

"I could arrange that."

He laughed. "You okay?"

"Yeah. I'm about to close up and go home."

"Good idea. Be careful. Call me if you have any trouble." That was nice. "You staying out of trouble?"

"Of course! I did hear from Franklin Polk yesterday, but nothing came of it." Oops. I realized I didn't want to tell him the whole story.

"Yeah?" His voice was alert.

I gave him the edited version. "So I tried to call him this morning, but he'd already left town."

"This car was trying to force you off the road?"

"I doubt it. You know how last night was. I was just spooked. It was nothing."

"You call me when you get home, okay?"

"I'll be fine!" I heard the edge in my voice. How many times had I said that today? He was just trying to be nice. "Really. But thanks."

"Yeah. Look, I think Julie's staying at her mom's tonight. No school tomorrow. Nights like this can get crazy, but" — he paused — "okay if I come by later if I get loose?"

"Sure."

"Okay. I'll, uh, see you later then."

"Yeah, see you later." Okay. Tonight I would definitely tell him about Kenneth Elliott and the twin paintings. He's homicide, not forgery or whatever that could be, but at least maybe he'd know what to do.

A few minutes later, the power went out. Tree limbs fallen across electric lines somewhere probably. Enough! I was going home.

It was slow, but I stuck to main roads that had been salted or sprayed with brine. Schools were closed, which took some of the traffic off the roads, but that meant a lot of parents were taking off early, too. It took an hour and a half to make the twenty-minute trip. By the time I exited on Music Valley Drive, my shoulders were in knots. I was looking forward to a hot, relaxing bath. Then I was going to turn on the fire and read. Detective Davis or not, I was getting into some flannel. Something soft and warm anyway. Maybe not flannel, maybe my new sweater. Blue. Like my eyes. Candles. Candles would be warm. And cozy.

The sleet had started, clicking softly on the windshield. It was fully dark now, and I was glad I was almost home. I passed the vacation condominiums and left all traffic behind. Then a car pulled out behind me. Where had it come from?

It looked like the same car from the night before.

I reached for my phone just as it hit me, slamming me forward. I bounced off the steering wheel, and the phone flew out of my hand. I tried to feel for it; it had landed in the passenger seat. I pulled it toward me and tried to punch the numbers, watch where I was going, and see what the big black car was doing, all at the same time. I pressed the buttons for Sam's number. It rang, and the car hit again. SLAM!

This time it wasn't just an icy hillside; the Cumberland River was below me. With rocks in between. He was pushing me now, relentless, my little Spider scooting along like dirt in front of a bulldozer. I kept trying

318

to steer away, but I couldn't evade him. I was bouncing over rocks closer and closer to the river bluff.

"Sam!" I yelled. "Sam! He's back. He's pushing me in the river!" I don't even know what I said. One more crunch, and the phone went flying again.

I got my foot back on the accelerator to give myself a little space, then twisted the wheel hard to the right. I tried to aim for a tree big enough to keep me out of the river. I saw trees flash by me as I hurtled downward; then I was headed straight for a large one. I hit it, and everything went black.

I don't think I was out for more than a few seconds, but I knew I had to get out of the car — and fast. Who was that guy? An irrelevant memory of Paul Newman and Robert Redford trying to outpace trackers flashed in my head. I knew that, whoever he was, he wouldn't give up now. He couldn't give up without making sure I couldn't tell anyone what had happened.

I flipped my seat belt off, opened the door, and fell into mud and wet leaves. I could hear his car above me, its headlights shining through the trees and into the dark space out over the river. The hill was steep enough at this point that the lights were overhead and might give me time to get away from my car. I rolled away from it, hoping I'd live long enough to know whether or not I was rolling in a patch of poison ivy.

The leaves were mostly off the trees, so the trees wouldn't provide much cover. The leaves underfoot were wet enough that they weren't making a lot of noise, but they were slippery. I tried to run, although my head hurt and my eyes were blurry. I couldn't see well, and I kept slipping in mud, running into trees and vines, and tripping. I lost a shoe and kept going. I was trying to run parallel to the road toward home or the first house I came to with lights on. Always go downhill when you're lost, my parents had told me on those long-ago trips to the Smokies. That's where civilization is. Go downhill and follow a running stream. But downhill was the Cumberland, and it would be a tough call whether I'd freeze first or drown there.

He must have had a flashlight, because now in addition to the lights from his car shining into the trees above me, a light was also moving around me. I tried to hide. Did he have a gun? I dropped behind a fallen tree and stayed still. The damp chill was soaking through my clothes; I couldn't feel the toes of my shoeless foot. I tried to wiggle them. I knew I needed to be able to run without stumbling. I kicked off the other shoe for better balance.

"Campbell?" A man was yelling my name. I couldn't get the fog out of my head now. I knew the voice. Doug? Was it Doug? I almost called out to him. But something wasn't right. Not Doug. Doug wouldn't hurt me, would he? Kenneth?

The light moved on, and I got up and ran. Like a stage spotlight, it came back, found me, and I could hear him in the trees. This chase seemed to go on forever. My head was throbbing. He was gaining on me. I slipped. I got up and tried to run and heard a siren in the distance. How far? Had Sam gotten my message? I had to keep going.

The siren grew louder. I could hear cars on the road above and to my left, but he was close enough that I could also hear his rasping breath. Or was that mine? It was hard to tell. My blood was pounding in my ears.

Something hit my shoulder, and I realized he was trying to hit me with his flashlight. He too was slipping in the mud and leaves.

"Why?" I gasped. "Why are you doing this?"

"You thought I'd just let you blackmail me. Easy money, huh? Everybody wants a piece of it. You're not going to ruin it for all of us. Not, hunnh, not after all this time."

I dodged sideways, anything to buy some time. I was dazed and exhausted, and I knew I couldn't last much longer. But one phrase stuck in my mind. All of us.

Just then I fell, and Kenneth Elliott lunged for me. I rolled; he slipped and went farther past me.

I scrambled to get up. He was turning back to me when my hand found a tree branch. I grabbed it. He was reaching for me when I remembered the self-defense demonstration I'd seen on the news. *The head is a difficult target. Go for the arms and shoulders, soft targets. You want to cause pain, not kill.* I shook my head to clear it. *Keep your eye on the ball and watch it all the way in. You're not trying to kill the ball; just make contact.* It was my brother's voice in the backyard repeating what he'd learned at Little League practice. *Level swing, just a good level swing.*

I swung as hard as I could. I missed the soft targets, but I connected with his head. I heard an unpleasant noise as the branch made contact, a sickening sound. He slumped to the ground.

I crawled back up the hill, climb two, slip one, to where my car was wedged headfirst into a tree. The door hung open. I reached in, feeling around for my phone. I was afraid to get into the car, afraid my weight would dislodge it and send it sliding down the hill. My fingers touched the phone, and I pulled it to me.

Nine-one-one.

I lay back in the freezing leaves. My head pounded, but I was grateful to be alive to feel the pain in my head and the sleet on my face.

Sirens. I heard sirens. Beautiful, lovely sirens. And getting closer this time.

"Police!" I could hear the sound of men scrambling in the underbrush above.

"Give it up, Elliott! It's over!"

It was Sam. Sam! I tried to call his name, but all I could do was wheeze.

Lights were flashing in the trees. Then one flashed off the car, and I lifted a hand, trying to wave.

"Over here. She's down. Over here."

Flashlights converged on me, alone in a spotlight.

"He's down there," I croaked.

"Ma'am? Ma'am? Are you hurt?"

"I hit him. I didn't want to kill him, but I had to stop him."

He turned to yell to another dark shape. "Down there. A man. May be injured."

The dark shape moved down the hill until

his light found Kenneth. I saw a glint of metal. I realized it was a police officer, and he was snapping handcuffs on Kenneth. He must not be dead, I thought. Surely they wouldn't put handcuffs on a dead man.

In seconds there were police and flashing lights — red, blue, yellow, white — all around me, and someone was helping me climb up the rest of the slope toward the road. Sam took my arm, which I realized also hurt, and looked in my eyes. "Are you all right?"

I blinked and tried to speak, but I started crying.

"Get her some help," he said roughly, and moved on.

At the road, I realized that at least one of the sirens must have been from an ambulance. Paramedics were asking me questions faster than I could think and wrapping me in a blanket. I heard a voice say, "Concussion, I think, maybe shock."

Lights were flashing, and radios were crackling. I was trying to focus on the red-haired paramedic's fingers in front of my eyes when I heard Doug's voice. "Campbell, are you okay? What happened?" I frowned, opened my mouth, and he said, "No. Don't tell me now." Good. I really didn't want to tell him I might have killed his brother.

Then police were crashing through the brush, shoving Kenneth Elliott in front of them. Sam Davis followed. Kenneth looked dazed and grim, and there was blood on the side of his head. But he was walking. Kenneth started to speak to Doug, but Doug said, "Don't say anything," and I realized that the lawyer had taken over.

"We're on our way downtown, Mr. Elliott," Sam said to Doug, "and we're going to want to ask you some questions, too. You want to ride with us, or will you come in your own car?"

"I'll be right behind you." He turned to his brother. "Don't say a word. I'll be right there."

Sam turned to me, and I started crying again. "My car, my little Spider." I fell toward him, and he put his arms around me.

"I'm sorry." His voice was rough. "We'll take a look at the car. We'll see. You need to get to a hospital now. I'll see you there later." He handed me off to a paramedic.

I couldn't seem to stop crying. As the paramedics led me to the ambulance, I could see the wrecker pulling up to take my Spider away.

Chapter Nineteen

But now that I'm older, just a little bit wiser,
I know what's important to do.
Don't need to prove nothin'; I know why I
   came here;
I just want to be here with you.

                — Jake Miller,
     "I Just Want to Be Here with You"

Don't go to an emergency room if you can help it, especially on an icy night, but if you do, go with a police escort. Even so, it seemed I waited hours in a cold, stark examining room before an adolescent doctor announced that I had a concussion and they would admit me for observation. I didn't want to be observed; I wanted to go home and go to bed.

Nurses came in regularly, shining tiny flashlights into my eyes. Once, when they woke me, I saw Sam across the room, slumped in a chair with his head in his hands. MaryNell was in another chair. It must have been nearing morning, because there was a faint light from the windows.

"Sam?"

"Yeah, I'm here."

I went back out.

I woke up later with a splitting headache. I managed to eat without throwing up. I had discovered that sounds and light made my head hurt worse. So did trying to think.

"Rosie Layne sent you flowers." MaryNell pointed to an arrangement of lilies on the window ledge. Rosie Layne, I reflected, was truly a lady. "Do you know what happened?"

I shook my head.

MaryNell was speaking quietly. "Doug Elliott confronted his brother about the painting in the Smith Logan museum brochure. Kenneth knew you'd recognized it as the original of the forged painting in Hazel Miller's house. Especially, I gather, after he caught you coming out of his back room," she explained. "What were you thinking?" I didn't answer. I was trying to remember. Smith Logan museum. Note cards. And Kenneth Elliott's back room. Forged!

"I think Franklin Polk had helped him forge some of the documentation on the paintings," MaryNell continued. "They'd

327

been doing this for years. It's how Hazel was getting by. And Polk and Kenneth weren't doing too badly themselves. Stick dropped by this morning and brought you this." She handed me a CD. *The Greatest Hits of Jake Miller, Volume Two.* I wished I could laugh without feeling like my head was the inside of one of Stick's drums.

All those calls, when I had persisted in trying to get Kenneth's evaluation of the museum, had sounded like extortion to him. Then, of course, he'd seen me sneaking out of his workroom. Then I'd had to go and talk to Doug, had to be fair.

MaryNell had been with me from the time Sam had called her, so she didn't know anything about my car. And cars were wrecked and off in ditches all over town. The first ice storm of the winter.

Sam had come by after questioning Kenneth for hours, but he had gone again. He asked MaryNell to tell me he'd be in touch. I would have to give a more complete statement. My head hurt.

"Was Franklin Polk trying to kill me, too? Did he know what Kenneth was doing?" And Doug. Did Doug know?

"Polk's still out of town, but he told Sam he has no idea what any of this is about. That he'd said you could come to his house, but you never showed. He didn't know what happened to you. Sam expects phone records will show he called Kenneth after he talked to you."

But Kenneth was already following me, I realized. The car I'd seen pulling out behind me. And the next night he waited for me on my way home.

"I don't think anybody knows for sure right now. But Polk was probably part of it. He said he was going to call the next day and see why you didn't show up, but he had an early flight."

When she was sure that I was conscious and going to be okay, MaryNell left to change clothes and go to work. I closed my eyes. My vision was better, but it was still blurry, and trying to see made my head hurt worse. I tried to think if I had any final payment or ticketing deadlines at work.

Randy called. It seemed a year since I'd left him outside Jimmy Kelly's. "I probably should pick you up next time." I started to laugh, but it made my head hurt too much.

Around lunchtime, Doug called. "Look, I can't talk to you about this. I shouldn't be calling at all. I won't be representing Kenneth in court; I've found him somebody who's good in criminal law. But it wouldn't be appropriate for me to talk to you about it. I just wanted to say that I'm sorry."

Yeah, well, sorry and $1.65 will buy you a cup of coffee.

By midafternoon, the doctors had decided to dismiss me. MaryNell picked me up on her way home and tucked me in on my couch with hot tea and chicken-noodle soup, the universal cure.

It was seven when Sam knocked at my door. He was carrying a pizza; a six-pack of Cokes; a cellophane-wrapped, grocery-store bunch of flowers; and a sack. He looked as if he hadn't slept in days.

"I thought you might be ready for some solid food. Pizza's the perfect food, you know. All four major food groups. You've got your bread, your meat. You've got cheese for your dairy. And vegetables: you've got tomatoes, tomato sauce, onions, peppers, and olives. It's all here." He held up the sack. "And Julie made you some chocolate-chip cookies, prescription-strength chocolate." He insisted I go back to the couch while he put the flowers in a tall glass of water and rummaged in my kitchen for plates, glasses and ice, forks, and paper towels in lieu of napkins.

"Why is it there's never a policeman around when you need one?" I asked as he settled on the floor in front of the couch.

"Must be because you seem to need one so often. We were onto him, you know. I told you we had a tire print. We compared it with everyone involved in the Miller case, and it matched his tires. Problem was, it didn't prove anything. A lot of people in Nashville have those tires. There was some suspicion of the forgery scheme, but what little information that division of the department had was pretty vague. It wasn't until Hazel's will was released, leaving all her paintings to Elliott, that the guy in that division made the connection."

I told him about the phone call from Polk and the St. Louis museum and the brochure I had sent to Kenneth. I told him what Kenneth had said when he was chasing me, although that was already in my statement. I told him about the painting in the workroom. He kept shaking his head.

"You don't think you should have told me about that?" His jaw hardened.

"Maybe."

"That still doesn't explain what you were doing going to meet a murder conspirator so late at night in the middle of nowhere." Sam was angry.

I tried to be reasonable. "I didn't have any reason to believe Franklin Polk was mixed up in murder. And I wasn't going to meet him in some deserted place. He asked me to come to his home. I was beginning to realize there was something fishy with the paintings, but I couldn't believe that Doug's brother could be a murderer. Please don't tell me Doug was part of this."

He shrugged. "Kenneth Elliott didn't know exactly how much you knew, but he thought you had figured out that he had sold paintings to Hazel back when she had more money, copied them and sold the originals for her, splitting the money with her. Eventually he had sold most of the forgeries, too, to buyers who had more money than sense, forging the provenances with Hazel's cooperation and, we think, Franklin Polk's. People didn't ask a lot of questions when they could tell their friends they'd bought art from Jake Miller's widow. It was a pretty good racket."

"So that's how Hazel had kept going all those years when the income from the trust wasn't enough to support Jake Miller's widow's lifestyle," I mused.

"Yep. Kenneth had counted on the originals not being seen publicly, and he purposely chose minor painters. He told us a little before your lawyer friend convinced him to be quiet."

My lawyer friend? Did I have a lawyer

friend anymore?

"Hazel wanted more money, but Kenneth thought the operation was getting too risky. More people are traveling and going to museums in other places far from home. Museums trade exhibits. A trip like the one you were planning is the perfect example. Internet exposure, too, was increasing the likelihood that someone would recognize a painting that wasn't where it was expected to be. Everything had changed since they started this soon after Jake's death. But Hazel was threatening to expose him if he didn't continue, and, in fact, raise the stakes."

"And the will, Hazel's will?"

"With the paintings going to Elliott and Franklin Polk as the executor, I suppose they all figured no one else would be likely to be examining the paintings."

"So how did he do it?"

"He knew Hazel regularly took sedatives. Who didn't? He was counting on the fact that everyone knew that, that most people would assume that she wouldn't be too picky about which ones she took. He came in from the back alley, counting on you and your lawyer friend to keep the house staff occupied as you reclaimed the paintings. He knew Hazel generally took naps in the afternoon, maybe chemically assisted. He got several extra pills down her dissolved in whiskey, apparently, then got impatient, we think. He held a pillow over her face until she was gone. Then he slipped out the French doors, not even knowing Jay Miller was out front providing an extra distraction. He must have thought he was incredibly lucky."

"How could he do that to his own brother?"

He shrugged. "He probably expected that Doug wouldn't be alone in the house."

"Was she dead when I saw her?"

"Probably."

Kenneth hadn't admitted all this; Doug had seen to that. But Sam was confident they'd get a conviction. There was some supporting physical evidence. "We found some prints in Hazel's bedroom we think are a match for Kenneth's, although it'll take a while for the lab to confirm that. A bottle of the same medication that was found in Hazel's bloodstream — with the same prints — was in a bank safe-deposit box registered to George Lewis."

"You've had all that all this time?"

"What did you think we were doing, sitting back waiting for you to figure this out for us? I kept telling you to stay out of it, leave it to us. But not the prescription bottle. We didn't have that until after Lewis was killed. When we started investigating Lewis's murder and opened his safe-deposit box, we found the medicine bottle in an envelope with a note. The note just had Kenneth Elliott's name on it. And there was also the art scheme. We hadn't put that together, but we were beginning to."

"Why didn't you say something, do something?"

He stopped and looked at me for a long minute, then laughed and shook his head.

"We had the prints from Hazel's room," he said, "but we didn't have any of Elliott's for a comparison. Even the prints wouldn't prove he had killed her, only that he had been in her room at some point in time. We didn't have enough to go on to bring him in. Nobody had placed him at the scene. And I had no idea you were going to be wearing a bull's-eye. Kenneth Elliott started out saying he lost control while driving, that he had no idea it was you, but I think we have too much for that to convince anyone. You'll have to testify, though."

"And he killed George Lewis?"

"That one's going to be harder to prove. No physical evidence so far. That bottle in the safe-deposit box goes a long way to proving motive, though. It seems Lewis tried to blackmail Kenneth Elliott and got himself murdered. Probably explains Lewis's sudden prosperity. Sudden and temporary. I doubt if we'll tie Polk to either Hazel's or Lewis's murder, but we may connect him to the extortion and your attempted murder. Remember the maid was supposed to go work for him."

"Doug wasn't part of this, was he?"

"We don't know for sure yet," Sam answered grudgingly. *Please, no.* "But we don't think so."

I could imagine how Doug was feeling about this — guilty, embarrassed, angry. If Doug hadn't allowed me to go with him to Hazel's that afternoon, I wouldn't have been involved at all. Kenneth was, after all, his brother, and I was much too involved in all that was being exposed about him. It might not help to shoot the messenger, but Doug wouldn't want to be too friendly with me anytime soon.

Sam turned to look me in the eye. "How much does that matter to you?"

I reached for a chocolate-chip cookie and realized that my answer to Sam's question could be very important. I thought about it for a minute, surprised to realize that it didn't matter the same way it might have a

336

few weeks ago.

I spoke carefully. "He's a friend. I'd be very disappointed in him — and, in a weird way, in myself — if he had known about this."

Sam nodded slowly.

"And Jake," I said. "What happened to Jake?"

"I don't imagine we'll ever know for sure. He could have stopped at some tavern. It was a long road. If what Rosie said is true, he had a lot on his mind. Maybe he was going to leave Hazel after all. If Hazel was with him on the drive back from Louisville after he'd talked with Rosie, maybe he told her the truth about Jacqueline, that he wanted a divorce to marry Rosie. Maybe Hazel didn't want to let that happen. What was she if she wasn't Jake Miller's wife? He was in trouble. And the way the stories go, when there was trouble, he went to a bottle." Sam shrugged.

"If Hazel did have anything to do with Jake's death, no wonder she was so mad when the will was read. Still, it's sad, somehow, not to know what definitely happened."

Sam nodded.

"What about my car?"

His face fell. "I'll be honest with you. It doesn't look good. MaryNell told me where you have it serviced, and we had it towed there. I thought the guy was going to cry. He said to tell you he'll do his best."

I closed my eyes and tried not to cry. It was just a car.

"Hey, none of that," he said. "You're okay. You only got hit in the head, and I've never seen a head any harder than yours. Have some pizza before it gets cold. You like anchovies?"

My head was hurting again, but I did like anchovies. And I could get to like a man who brought me anchovy pizza and chocolate-chip cookies.

ACKNOWLEDGEMENTS

Thank you to the wonderfully patient and helpful folks at Thomas Dunne Books, especially editors Hannah Braaten, Melanie Fried, and Jennifer Letwack, and copy editor Mary-Ann Johanson. Thanks, too, to my invaluable resource and agent, Jill Marr. Thank you to my family and friends who have read early drafts and encouraged me for years, to David, Mom, who took me downtown on her lunch hour to buy Nancy Drew books, and Dad, who first taught me to love country music, Mike, Mark and Wendy, Colin, Nathan, and Evan, to Shawn and Brandon, Pat and Paul, to Dr. Constance Fulmer, to Barbara, Pam, Melinda, and Betty, to Frances, Judy, Suzanne, Karol, Julie, Debbie, Gale, Margaret, Leah, Paula, Mark, Greg, and so many more. Thanks to the Pokeno group, to the Bodacious Books critique group: Mary Saums, Rai-lyn Wood, Mary Richards, J. T. Ellison, Del Tinsley, Jill

Thompson, Cecilia Tichi, Janet McKeown, and Dee Lambert, who first invited me. Thank you to the students from whom I've learned so much, and thank you to Mrs. Barrett, Mrs. Tyler, and all my other inspiring teachers. I hope they knew how important they were to the little girl who talked too much in class.

ABOUT THE AUTHOR

Peggy O'Neal Peden grew up in Middle Tennessee and has lived in and around Nashville for most of her life. She has taught English at high school and college levels, owned a travel agency, been published in regional magazines, and written award-winning advertising copy. She is a member of the Nashville Artist Guild and lives in Nashville. *Your Killin' Heart* is her first novel.

The employees of Thorndike Press hope you have enjoyed this Large Print book. All our Thorndike, Wheeler, and Kennebec Large Print titles are designed for easy reading, and all our books are made to last. Other Thorndike Press Large Print books are available at your library, through selected bookstores, or directly from us.

For information about titles, please call:
(800) 223-1244

or visit our website at:
gale.com/thorndike

To share your comments, please write:
Publisher
Thorndike Press
10 Water St., Suite 310
Waterville, ME 04901